Rocco cupped her face and bent down for a kiss.

Slower, softer, but still a kiss that killed her. He tilted his brow to rest it on hers and held her close in his arms. Francesca felt the heat, the strength, the fire of this man all around her.

'I want you so badly. I want you like I've never wanted any other woman. Ever.'

He pushed back from her, still held her head, stayed nose to nose with her.

'You are with me now. The games are over.'

He kissed her again, fiercely branded her mouth with his tongue. Then he stepped back, ran one hand through his hair and took her hand in the other.

'Come. We will go to my home.'

Unable to sit still without reading, **Bella Frances** first found romantic fiction at the age of twelve, in between deadly dull knitting patterns and recipes in the pages of her grandmother's magazines. An obsession was born! But it wasn't until one long, hot summer, after completing her first degree in English literature, that she fell upon the legends that are Mills & Boon® books. She has occasionally lifted her head out of them since to do a range of jobs, including barmaid, financial adviser and teacher, as well as to practise (but never perfect) the art of motherhood to two (almost grown-up) cherubs. Bella lives a very energetic life in the UK, but tries desperately to travel for pleasure at least once a month—strictly in the interests of research!

Catch up with her on her website at bellafrances.co.uk

Other books by Bella Frances

Modern Tempted™

Dressed to Thrill

Visit the author profile page at
millsandboon.co.uk for more titles

THE PLAYBOY
OF ARGENTINA

BY
BELLA FRANCES

MILLS
BOON

Published in Great Britain 2015
by Mills & Boon, an imprint of Harlequin (UK) Limited,
Eton House, 18-24 Paradise Road, Richmond, Surrey, TW9 1SR

© 2015 Bella Frances

ISBN: 978-0-263-24902-6

Harlequin (UK) Limited's policy is to use papers that are natural,
renewable and recyclable products and made from wood grown in
sustainable forests. The logging and manufacturing processes conform
to the legal environmental regulations of the country of origin.

Printed and bound in Spain
by CPI, Barcelona

THE PLAYBOY
OF ARGENTINA

For my mother, with all my love.

CHAPTER ONE

IN THE LAZY warmth of a summer afternoon, Rocco 'Hurricane' Hermida stepped out of his helicopter onto the utterly perfect turf of the Buenos Aires Campo Argentino de Polo. From her vantage point in the crowd Frankie Ryan felt the air around her ripple with the flutter of a thousand eyelashes. If awe was a sound it was the reverent silence of grown men turning to stare at their own demigod. No doubt the polo ponies were stamping and snuffling and shaking their shaved manes adoringly, too. Yet all *she* could feel were the unbidden tremors of hurt and humiliation and—damn him to hell—shame.

With every step he took across the springy grass his fabulous outline sharpened. A little taller, definitely more muscular. Could his hair be longer? It had seemed so shockingly defiant all those years ago. Now it just trademarked him as none other than Argentina's own—her finest, proudest export.

Wind whipped at silk skirts and hands flew to hair and hats. The crowd swelled and leaned closer. For a second her view was obscured, but then there he was again. Clearer and nearer. Ruggedly, shockingly beautiful. And still making her heart pound in her ears—after all these years.

He turned, cast his profile; it was caught on camera

and screened all around. The scar through his eyebrow and the break in his nose—still there. A hand landed on his shoulder, and then there at his side was his brother Dante, as blond as Rocco was dark—twin princes of Darkness and Light.

It really was breathtaking. Just as they said in the media. Only even more potent in the flesh. The dazzling smiles of their happy conspiracy, the excitement of the match, the thrill of the crowd. How intoxicating.

How sickening.

How on earth was she going to get through the next four hours? The party afterwards, the gushing hero-worship? All over the man who had looked her in the eye, kissed her full on the mouth and broken her soft, trusting heart.

Easy. It would be no problem at all. How hard could it be to watch a little polo, sip a little Pimm's and keep well out of trouble?

Tipping too large sunglasses onto her too small nose, she took a seat on the high-rise bleachers and crossed her jiggling legs. Maybe she shouldn't have come here today. She could so easily have made this stopover in Buenos Aires and not taken in a polo match. It wasn't as if she was obsessed with the game itself. Not anymore.

Sure, she'd grown up more in a stable than in a home. And yes, once upon a time becoming a polo player had been her sixteen-year-old heart's desire. But she'd been naive back then. Naive enough to think her father had been kidding when he said the best thing she could hope to become was a rich man's secretary, or better still a rich man's wife. And even more naive to throw herself into the arms of the most dashing man she'd ever seen and almost beg him to take her to bed.

Almost beg? That wasn't strictly accurate, either.

At least in the ten years since then she'd got well past palpitations and hand-wringing.

She spread out her pale Celtic skinny fingers, frowned them steady. Looked at the single silver ring with *Ipanema* carved in swirling writing—a gift for her fourteenth birthday, worn ever since. She rubbed at it. She still missed that pony. And she still hated the man who had stolen her away.

But at least Ipanema's line was alive and well. She was the dam of two of the ponies on Rocco Hermida's string. His favourites, as he made no secret of telling the world's press. And rumoured to be being used in his groundbreaking genetics programme. *And* about to carry him onto the field and to victory at this charity polo match. Well, that was what everyone here thought any-way. To the home crowd there was not a shred of doubt that Argentina's darling was going to triumph over the Palm Beach team. Totally. Unquestionably. And, with his brother at his side, the crowd would be guaranteed eight chukkas of the most mouthwatering display of virile man candy in the whole of South America.

But Frankie Ryan wasn't drooling or licking her lips. Oh, no.

She was rolling her eyes and shaking her head. As much at herself for her stupid reaction—thankfully she now had that under *total* control—as at the flirty polo groupies all around her.

The fact that Rocco Hermida was here, playing, was completely irrelevant. It really was.

He probably didn't even remember her…

Which was actually the most galling thing of all. While she had burned with shame and then fury on learn-ing that he'd bought Ipanema, and had then been sent off to the convent, *he* had appeared in her life like a meteor, blazed a trail and as quickly blazed off. He'd never been back in touch. He'd taken her pride and then her joy. But she had learned a lesson. Letting anyone get under her skin like that was never going to happen again.

She had a perfectly legitimate reason for being here that had nothing to do with Rocco Hermida. She might look like a tourist today, but she was full of business. Landing a job as product development manager at Evaña Cosmetics, after slogging her guts out as an overgrown intern and then an underpaid assistant just so she could sock it to her old man was a dream come true!

She could think of worse things than travelling to the Dominican Republic and then Argentina in search of the perfect aloe vera plantation. And she could think of much worse things than an overnighter in Buenos Aires to lap up the polo followed by a weekend at her friend Esme's place in Punta del Este to lap up the sun and the sea.

Bliss.

She got another drink—why not? As long as she was fresh enough to start on her presentation tomorrow she could have a little downtime today. It might even do her good to relax before she went out on her last trips. She still had plenty of time to put it all together into a report before the long flight home and her moment in the boardroom spotlight.

It was *such* a big deal. She'd spent so long convincing the directors to take this leap of faith, to look farther than their own backyard for organic ingredients, to have a unique selling point that was *truly* unique. So while she could play the tourist here today, the last thing she'd do was jeopardise it by getting all caught up in Rocco damn Hermida.

She began to thread and weave through the contrasting mix of casual *porteños* and glamorous internationals. On the other side of the giant field, spread out like bunting, she spotted the exclusive white hospitality tents. Esme would be in one of them, playing hostess, smiling and chatting and posing for pictures. As the Palm Beach captain's wife, she was part of the package. Frankie could imagine nothing worse.

An announcement rang like a call to prayer, and another headshot loomed on the giant screens. There he was again. The default scowl back in position, the dark hair swept back and landing in that flop across his golden brow. He was in the team colours, scarlet and black, white breeches and boots. As the camera panned out, she instinctively looked at his thighs. Under the breeches they were hard, strong and covered in the perfect dusting of hair. She knew. She remembered. She'd kissed them.

For a moment she felt dazed, lost in a mist of girlish memories. Her first crush, her first kiss, her first broken heart. All thanks to that man. She drew her eyes off the screen again, scowled at it. Muttered words under her breath that her mother would be shocked to hear, let them slide into the wind with the commentator's jabbering biography—a 'what's not to love?' on the Hurricane— and the brassy notes of a gaudy marching band.

The first chukka was about to start. The air around her sparkled with eager anticipation. She could take her place—she could watch this—and if he turned her stomach with his arrogance she could cheer on Palm Beach. Even if two of his ponies *were* from Ipanema, the Rocco Hermida on those screens was just an imprint of a figment of a teenage girl's infatuation. She owed him nothing.

If only it was that simple.

He was electric.

Each chukka was more dramatic and stunning than the one before.

He galloped like the wind and turned on a sixpence. His scowl was caught on camera, a picture of composed concentration, and when he scored—which he did, ten times—a flash of white teeth was his momentary gift to the crowd.

And of course there was Dante, too. Like a symphony, they flew up and down the field. Damn, damn, *damn*, but it was utterly, magnetically mesmerising.

They won. Of course. And as fluttering blue-and-white flags transformed the stadium and the crowd hollered its love she scooted her way out. Head down, her face a picture of 'seen it all before, can take it or leave it, nothing that special', she made her way round to the ponies—the real reason she was here.

The grooms were hosing down the last of them when she slipped through the fence, and watery arcs of rainbows and silvery droplets filled the air. She sneaked around, watched the action. She loved this. She missed it. Until this moment she hadn't realised how much.

Everyone was busy, the chat was lively and the whole place was buzzing at the fabulous result. Of course the Palm Beach team were no pushovers, and Esme would be satisfied, but the day belonged to Rocco Hermida. And Dante. As expected.

As soon as she had taken a little peep at the two ponies she wanted to see she'd head off, have a soak in the tiny enamel bath in her hotel's en-suite bathroom. She would use some of the marketing gifts from the last plantation: a little essential oil to help her relax, and a little herbal tea to help her sleep. She'd been on the go for twenty-four hours. Even if she did make the party tonight, which

Esme seemed so determined she would, sleep was going to have to feature somewhere.

No one was paying her any attention. She didn't blame them. Small and slight and unremarkable, she tended to pass under most people's radar. Unlike the polo scene groupies, who were just like the ponies—all perfect teeth, lean bodies and long legs. Treated as a boy until she'd realised herself that being a girl was a lot more fun, she'd run with her brothers, ridden the horses and wandered wild and free all over the farm. Until the day that she had flown out of the stables to hunt for her brothers and run straight into Rocco Hermida.

She would never forget that moment.

Rounding the corner, she'd seen him, blazing like sunshine after thunder in the shadows of the muddy lane. He'd stood and stared. She'd slammed to a stop and gawped at him. She had never seen anything more brilliant, more handsome, more menacing. He'd looked her over, taken his time. Then he'd turned back to Mark and Danny and wandered away, rattling off questions in his heavily accented English, turning her life on its head, oblivious.

Now he was responsible for this world-class string of ponies, his world-class genetics programme and a whole host of other businesses. But polo was his passion. Everyone knew that. And the giant horse transporter with 'Hermanos Hermida' on it, parked at the rear of the *campo* and drawing her closer, was an emblem of how much care he put into his ponies.

It was immaculate. A haven. Ponies were hosed down, dried off and resting in their stalls. Gleaming and proud. She walked amongst them, breathing in their satisfied air. Where were her girls? She was so keen to see the mix of thoroughbred and Argentinian pony, trained to world-class perfection. She knew she'd recognise Ipanema's progeny—the ponies he'd kept on the string were her living image. She felt sure she would feel some kind of connection with them.

'Que estas haciendo aqui?'

Right behind her. Frankie started at the quiet growl. Her stomach twisted. Her whole body froze.

'Did you hear me? I said, what are you doing?'

Words stuck, she willed herself calm. 'Just looking,' she finally managed.

'Turn round.'

She would not—could not.

'I said, turn round.'

If she'd been in the heart of an electric storm she couldn't have felt more charged. The voice she hadn't heard for years was as familiar as if he had just growled those unforgettable words, 'You are too young—get out of here!'

A pony turned its head and stared at her with a huge brown eye. Her heart thunder-pulsed in her chest. Her legs felt weak. But from somewhere she found a spark of strength. He might be the most imposing man she had ever known, but she was her own woman now—not a little girl. And she wouldn't let herself down again.

She turned. She faced him. She tilted up her chin.

He stared, took a pace towards her. Her heel twitched back despite herself.

'I knew it was you.'

She forced her eyes to his even as the low growl in his voice twisted around her.

He was still in his playing clothes, his face flushed with effort and sweat, his hair mussed and tousled. Alive and vital and male. She could hardly find the strength to stand facing him, eyeing him, but she was determined to hold her own in the face of all that man.

'I came to see Ipanema's mares.'

Her words were stifled and flat in the perfectly climate-controlled air. Another pony stamped and turned its head.

'You came to see *me*.'

Her eyes widened in shock and she spluttered a laugh. 'Are you joking?'

He stepped back from her, tilted his head as if she was a specimen at some livestock market and he might, just might, be tempted.

He raised an eyebrow. Shook his head—the slightest movement. 'No.'

He was appalling, arrogant—outrageous in his ego.

'Look, think what you like—and I'm sorry I didn't ask permission to come to a charity match—but, *really*? Come to see *you*? When I was sixteen I had more than my fill of you.'

A rush of something dangerous, wicked and wondrous flashed over his eyes and he closed the gap between them in a single step. His fingers landed on her shoulder, strong, warm and instantly inflaming. He didn't pull her towards him. He didn't need to. She felt as if she was flush against him, and her body sang with delight.

'You didn't get your fill—not at all.' He curled his lip for a moment. 'But you wanted to.'

The coal-black eyes were trained right on her and she knew if she opened her mouth it would be to whimper. She clamped it shut. She would stare him out and then get the hell away from him.

But his hand moved from her shoulder, spread its warming brand up her neck.

'Frankie… Little Frankie.'

He cupped the back of her head, held her. Just there.
She jerked away.

'What?'

If she could have spat out the word with venom she
would have, but she was lucky to get it out at all, the way
he was simply staring at her.

'All grown-up.'

He took another step. She saw the logo of his team in
red silk thread: two balls, two sticks, two letters *H*. She
saw the firm wall of muscle under his shirt—hard, wide
pecs, the shadow of light chest hair framed in the V. She
saw the caramel skin and the wide muscular neck, the
heavy pepper of stubble and the rich wine lips. She saw
his broken nose, his intensely dark eyes, his questioning
brows. And she scented him. Pure man.

That hand was placed on her head—and it felt as if
he was the high priest and this was some kind of heal-
ing ritual.

One she did not need to receive.

'Yes, all grown-up. And leaving.' She pulled away.
'Let me past. I want to go.'

But he held her. Loosely. His eyes finally dropped
to absorb every other possible detail. She could feel his
appraisal of her sooty eyes too big for her face; her nose
too thin; her mouth too small; her chin too pointed. But
instead of stepping back he seemed to swell into the last
remaining inch of space and he shook his head.

'In a moment. Where are you staying?'

She wavered—rushed a scenario through her mind
of him at her cute little hotel, in her tiny room. Filling
up all the space. The picture was almost too hot to hold
in her head.

'That doesn't matter. I'm only here for a day or so.'

He was in no hurry to move. She looked away, around,

at the empty glass she somehow still clutched in her hand. Anywhere but at him.

'I think you should stay a little longer. Catch up.'

There was nothing but *him*—his body and his energy. Ten years ago she had dreamed of this moment. She had wept and pined and fantasised. And now she would rather die than give him the satisfaction.

'Catch up with what? I've no wish to go over old ground with you.'

'You think we covered ground? Back then? In that tiny little bed in your farmhouse?'

His words slipped out silken and dark.

'You have no idea, *querida*, how far I would have liked to have gone with you.'

He caught a handful of her bobbed hair and tugged. She flinched—not in pain, but in traitorous delight.

'How far I would go with you now...'

He smoothed a look of hunger all over her face. And her whole body throbbed.

'You've got no chance,' she hissed.

A smile—just a flash. Then his mouth pursed in rebuttal. A shake of his head.

It was enough. She put her hands on him and shoved. Utterly solid—she hadn't a hope. He growled a laugh, but he moved. Stepped to the side.

His tone changed. 'Your horses are resting. They played well. In the stalls at the top. Take your time.'

She pushed past him, desperate to escape from this man, but two steps away she stopped.

She swallowed. 'Thank you.'

'The pleasure is mine, Frankie.' He whispered it, threatened it. 'And I aim to repeat it.'

He left her there. She didn't so much hear him go as feel a dip in the charge in the air. The ponies looked round at her—sympathising, no doubt, with how hard it was to share breathing space with someone who needed his own solar system.

She found her mares. Saw their Irish names—Roisin and Orla—and their white stars, but most of all their infamously wonderful natures, marking them out as Ipanema's. She could never criticise what he had done with them—the effort and love he poured into all of his stock was legendary. And she was proud that Ipanema's bloodlines were here, in one of the best strings in the world. If only Ipanema was still here, too…

Her brother Mark would be delighted. His own expertise was phenomenal in the field of equine genetics and this line had put their stud farm on the map. She knew he kept in touch with Rocco, sharing professional knowledge from time to time, while her father had fumed silently every time his name was mentioned. His suspicions had never been proved, but he'd never let her forget that he had them. Oh, no. And he'd punished her by sending her off to the convent to learn to 'behave'.

But she'd been away from Ireland five years now. Away from that life and forging her own. Madrid was her home; Evaña was her world. Her father had passed the business to Mark and all her contact with beautiful creatures like these was sadly limited to the infrequent trips she made to see him.

She kissed their polished necks and they whickered their appreciation, soothing her heated blood before she went back out into the day.

Sometimes animals were a lot easier to deal with than people. Actually, animals had *always* been easier than people. They had their moods and their own personalities, of course, but they never judged, never made her feel like the slightly gawky, awkward tomboy that everyone else did. Especially Ipanema. Being given her as a foal to bring on had changed her life completely.

She'd loved that pony, and Ipanema had loved her right back, and when she'd been sold to Rocco her heart had taken its first battering.

She stepped out into the warm afternoon. The thrill and roar of the crowd had died down, but the celebrations were only just beginning. There was to be a party at the Molina Lario Hotel later, hosted by the champagne sponsors. Esme had told her to join her there.

It's only the most talked-about event in the charity polo circuit after Dubai and Deauville! You need to let your hair down—there's more to life than work!

But Rocco would most likely be there. And her reserves were running low. Maybe she'd call it a day, lap up the night safe in bed and swerve the whole unfolding drama attached to seeing him again.

She pushed her glasses back up her nose and wound her way round to the flotilla of white hospitality tents, her legs more obedient, less shaky now. But she should have known better than to think she was home free. At the edge of the field and up on the screens were four tall men in red, black and white, four in blue and yellow. All were standing on the podium, and every eye was drawn to them. Even hers.

Round about them were all the beautiful people. She hung back, watched.

A cheer… The cup being passed over, held up. Dante beaming his easy, confident golden smile. Rocco curling his lip. The crowd adoring.

They stepped down and into the flow of people— mostly girls, she noticed. Well, they were nothing but obliging! Letting themselves get all wrapped up in them, posing together in a spray of champagne, moving to another little group. Another pose, a squeeze, kisses on cheeks.

She'd seen it all before, of course—most recently in the pages of various magazines and in online news. But watching it like this she felt a flame of anger burst inside her. Anger at herself for still being there! Still gawping. She was a respected businesswoman now. Not a stupid, infatuated little girl!

She turned and began a fast path out. She'd get a cab, get away, get her head straight.

Her flat-heeled sandals moved swiftly over the grass, her stride long in her cotton sundress. Molina Lario was getting less and less attractive by the moment. More of that? No, thanks. Esme would understand. She knew her feelings for the arrogant Rocco ran to pathological disgust—she just didn't know why.

No one did.

The one thing she could thank him for, she supposed, was igniting that fire for her to get the hell out of County Meath. When she'd watched him swing his rucksack over his shoulder and walk away from her, down the single-track farm lane, through the dawn light and rain dust, she'd realised he was heading back into a world wide open with choices and chances. She didn't need to be tied to County Meath, to Ireland, to the narrow options of which her dad thought her capable.

She'd taken a cold hard look at herself. Skinny, flat chested, unattractive and unkempt. Her dressing table cluttered with riding trophies instead of make-up. And when she'd stopped wailing and sobbing into her pillow she'd plotted her escape.

And now here she was—out in the world.

And here she would stay—proving them all wrong.

Head down, she reached the gates.

Just as a figure in black stepped alongside her. Large, male, reeking of strength.

'Señor Hermida asks that you join him.'

A rush…a thrill thrummed through her. For a moment she felt the excitement of flattery. Tempted.

But, no. That way disaster lay. She was headed in a whole different direction.

She didn't even break her step.

'Not today. Or any other day, thanks.'

She eyed the gate like a target board, upped her pace. Lost him.

Almost at the gate, she felt his presence again.

'Miss Ryan, Señor Hermida will collect you later for the party. 10:00 p.m. At your hotel.'

She spun on her heel, ready to fire a vicious volley of words right back. But he was walking away, obscured by the hundreds of people crossing in front of her. As obscured as her own feelings at seeing the Hurricane.

So sure he'd mean nothing to her, she'd turned up as if it was all in a day's work to bump into him. But skulking about in the crowds, sneaking among the horses when she could so easily have done things properly…? She should have asked Mark to set it up. That was what someone who truly wasn't fazed would have done—brushed off what had happened between them and joined him for a drink and a chat for old times' sake…

Instead of spontaneously combusting when he'd come up behind her.

He was dangerous. The last thing she needed.

Her career was her life. Not ponies. Or polo. Or dark, intense men who lit up her body and squeezed at her heart.

She emerged onto the pavement like a hostage set free. He didn't know her hotel. And he didn't know *her*.

Collect her later? Arrogant fool. One overbearing father and two extremely alpha brothers did *not* make Frankie Ryan anyone's pushover.

She would be swaddled in Do Not Disturbs and deep, deep sleep. He could just cross her off his list and move to the next name. There were bound to be hundreds.

CHAPTER TWO

'SO MANY GIRLS, so little time,' Dante mouthed, and winked at him over the heads of the two dancers from Rio who had just wound themselves around him.

Well, that was him taken care of for the evening—or the next couple of hours at least.

Rocco had just peeled a sweet little blonde from hm. Normally his preferences did run to sweet little blondes, but tonight… He strode to the wide windows that ran the length of the Art Hotel penthouse—Dante's go-to joint for post-match partying. Tonight he was well off his game.

He braced his hands on the glass and stared out across Palermo to the outskirts, where he knew her hotel was. One phone call and he'd found out everything he needed to know. One phone call that had confirmed she was in town long enough for him to scratch the itch that had started all those years ago.

The blonde put her arms around his waist again. He was losing patience with her, but she would be well looked after—by someone else.

He looked round at his team members and friends. All getting into the party spirit one way or another. For Rocco the party wouldn't start until he had Frankie Ryan in his arms. Then and only then would he get rid of this tension that had built almost to a frenzy since he'd seen her sneaking into the transporter.

He checked his watch.

Too early, but he had a feeling she wasn't going to be waiting on the steps of her hotel wearing an expectant look and a corsage. No, something told him that she was going to be a little less easy to convince than the now-sulking blonde, who'd finally realised he wasn't just playing hard to get.

He called his driver. He couldn't wait anymore.

'Dante—I will catch you up.'

His brother, busy, lifted an arm in acknowledgement. He hadn't told him he'd seen her at the match. Wasn't in the mood for questions. Why? Because he barely understood himself why this slip of a girl, now a woman, had occupied so much of his head for so long.

The last time Dante had raised the subject with him, after a particularly broody day in Dublin when he'd failed to make contact with her, it hadn't gone well. He'd called her Rocco's 'Irish obsession'. It was probably the only time they'd failed to agree on anything. He'd admit it now, though. He was definitely obsessing about her now.

He checked his phone, his money and, for the first time in a long time, his appearance. He knew how he looked. He wasn't coy or stupid. Normally it was irrelevant. There were far, far more important things in this world—like loyalty, like honour. Like family…

And if he was honest, that penthouse full of beautiful women back there…? None of them interested him more than the skinny, hazel-eyed Irish kid he'd met ten years earlier. A little bit of closure on that particular puzzle would be good—it had been a long time coming.

He swung into the back of the sedan. An hour earlier than he'd suggested and the city was limbering itself up for the night ahead. The party at Molina Lario would be good, for starters. But he was feeling post-match wired and just this side of in control. He spread his arms across the back of the seat, watched the sights of his town slip past. A bit of Barcelona here…a look of Paris there. The spill of people on wide streets, corners alive with café culture. Vibrant, creative and free.

But he was no romantic fool. Yes, he loved it. Loved it that he had run its streets and slept in its parks. Loved it that he had survived. Was grateful that he had survived when so many others had fallen or, perhaps worse, were living the legacy of those years in prisons or still on the streets. He would never, ever forget or take that for granted.

But all he had—his wealth, his businesses, his health, his adoptive family—all of that he would trade right now for one more day with Lodo. One more chance to shield him and protect him and cherish him—better than he'd managed last time…

The car cruised to a stop. They were here. He hadn't been in this part of town for years. Villa Crespo was outside Palermo and on the up, but he would have preferred that she'd stayed closer to the centre, where the worst that could happen was pickpocketing. He got out. Looked around. It seemed quiet enough. The hotel was traditional—a single frontage villa. Ochres and oranges. Cute, he supposed. He went inside.

The concierge was startled to see him, and he jumped up from his TV screen, gave him the details he needed. Her room, first floor; her visitors, none; and her movements, she'd been in her room since her return earlier.

He ignored the old cage elevator and took the stairs three at a time. If she felt about him the way he thought she did they could stay in her room. No problem. Or they could hang out for a while and then go on to another party, or back to Dante's pad, or even to the estancia. It had been a long time since he'd taken a woman back there. But he felt even now that one night with Frankie Ryan might not be enough. An undisturbed weekend? That might just about slake this thirst for her.

He stood outside her door.

Dark polished wood. Brass number five.

He knocked. Twice. Rapid. Impatient.

Nothing.

She should be getting ready, at the very least.

He knocked again.

Still nothing.

He'd opened his mouth to growl out her name when the door swung open.

And there she was.

Bleary eyed, hair mussed and messy, one bony white shoulder exposed by the slipped sleeve of her pale blue nightdress, her face screwed up against the light from the hall.

He'd never seen anything more adorable in his life.

'Frankie.'

He stepped forward, the urge to grab hold of her immense.

But she put a hand to her head, set her features to a scowl and opened her mouth in an incredulous O.

'What—what are *you* doing here?'

He still couldn't believe how sleepily, deliciously gorgeous she looked. His eyes roamed all over her—the eyemask now awry, the milky pale skin and the utter lack of anything under that thin jersey nightdress. It clung to her fine bones and tiny curves. As beguiling as he remembered, though maybe her breasts were rounder, fuller...

'What are you—? Why are you—? I told your guy I wasn't coming.'

He dragged his eyes back to her face. Heard a noise at the end of the corridor. The concierge was peeping, making an 'everything all right?' face, wielding a pass key. Rocco nodded, put up his hand to keep him back.

'Let me in, Frankie.'

She seemed almost to choke out her answer. 'No!'

'Okay, I'll wait here—get dressed.'

'I'm. Not. Coming.'

He was slightly amused. Slightly. The irony of the situation was not lost on him.

'We've been here before, *querida*, only last time it was you on the other side of the door. Remember?'

And there it was—that wildness he had seen all those years ago. That almost wantonness she'd exuded that he'd found exhilarating, intoxicating. She leaned out into the corridor, to check who was there, then looked right up at him. He drew his eyes away from the gaping lines of her nightdress, followed her gaze.

'I can't believe you're actually standing here!'

'It would be better if I came in. As I recall, that was your preference last time.'

'I was *sixteen*! I made a mistake!' She blazed out her answer.

Then she gripped her arms round herself. All that happened was that the neckline of her nightdress splayed open even more, letting him see right to the tip of one small high breast. He reached forward, gently lifted the fabric and tugged it back into position, ignoring her futile attempts to swat his arm away.

'Why don't we discuss that inside?'

His hand hovered, then retracted. He badly wanted to touch her, but he was nothing if not a reader of women and he sensed she was going to need more than a pep talk to get her on-message.

'You made yourself perfectly plain the last time we met. And I don't have any wish to spend any more time with you. I *told* your guy. I couldn't have been plainer.'

'The last time we met was four hours ago. You were in my horse transporter. You came looking for me.'

She was so wild, standing there in next to nothing. He was getting harder and harder just looking at her. Memories came of her slipping into his bed, waking him up with her naive little kisses and her hot little body. Him literally pushing her out of his bed—like rejecting heaven.

Her eyes blazed. 'I came looking for our bloodline, not *you*! You arrogant ar—'

He put his finger on her lips where they framed the word he knew she was about to launch at him. Her eyes widened even more.

'Don't belittle yourself, *querida*.' He lowered his voice, stepped closer. 'Go inside, get dressed, and I will take you to the party and tell you everything you want to know about your ponies.'

But lightning-quick she grabbed for his hand and tried to pull it away. The sleeve of her nightdress fell lower and the pull of the fabric strained on her breasts. Her nipples, twin buds, drew his eyes—and, damn it, the flame of heat coursed straight to his groin.

'I call it as I see it, and I see you as an—'

He couldn't hold back. She fired him, inflamed him. He wanted to taste her so badly. He had to contain her, have her mouth under his.

She lifted her arms to push him and he scooped her wrists together, pinned them behind her. Then he heaved her against him and crushed her insolent mouth. Fragile but strong, she strained and stiffened and held her lips closed. Which just drove him wilder! He could smell her desire. He could taste her passion. So why was she so intent on keeping him back?

He gripped her head and stared into her eyes.

Her hands flew to his wrists. She dug in her nails. She flashed and fumed and forced out her breath through the clenched teeth in her mouth. But she didn't pull back, and he needed to *know*. He grabbed her hips and ground her into his hard, throbbing length, felt her sweet mound and watched her shocked face.

And he saw. Oh, yes. *Oh. Yes.* She told him. Her eyes closed. Her head dropped back and she moaned. Dark and deep and long.

That was it. All he needed to know.

He thrust her away, spun her round, slapped her backside.

'Get in there. Get dressed. Meet me outside. You have half an hour.'

He'd had to get back onto the street—get some air. Calm his blood.

So he'd been right all these years when he'd wondered if he was idolising a memory. If she really had fired him up as fast and hard as his youthful body had ever experienced.

He really should have been given a medal after that weekend. The utterly overt way she'd tried to seduce him had been sweet, but he doubted her family had thought so. And they hadn't known the half of it.

From the first moment when he'd seen her in filthy jodhpurs to her sidling up beside him at dinner as he'd tried to keep focussed on the deal he was supposed to be there to cut with her brother, her face covered in make-up she'd clearly had no notion of how to apply, and wearing a dress—which had seemed to cause her family some amusement. To the full-blown assault of her coming into his room.

Kiss me, Rocco.

That look in her eyes…the shadow between her open wet lips. He had wanted to—so badly. She'd blown his mind. But of course he had chased her away. What kind of guy took advantage of a girl five years younger, barely aware of her own sexuality, acting as if she'd never even been kissed? And there was the fact that her family's hospitality to him had been beyond reproach… She was off limits, and then some.

But in the predawn light she'd woken him again. Naked. In his bed. The memory still packed a punch.

He had been disorientated, but harder than he had ever thought possible. Seconds, maybe minutes had passed as they'd found each other, and he'd done things he should never have done. But thank God he had stopped in time—before it had gotten out of hand. She had begged and wailed and made it even harder for him to send her away. So in the end he'd left himself. After one look back at her, wrapped in a sheet, all eyes and white skin. One look that he had never erased from his mind.

He pushed up off the sedan's door, walked, paced down the street. He had already drawn attention to himself. He should be waiting in the car. A crowd was starting to gather—people who were wondering what the hell the captain of the polo team that had just won the biggest charity match ever seen in Palermo was doing, tonight of all nights, outside a midrange hotel in Villa Crespo.

He checked his watch.

Forty minutes.

And then he knew.

She wasn't coming.

He stared up at the first-floor windows. Maybe a curtain twitched.

The throng of interested happy people watched and waited. The concierge wrung his hands at the door.

Rocco turned away from the crowd. Got into the car. Nodded to his driver and was driven off through the streets.

What kind of stupid game was she playing? They had unfinished business. A hot physical agenda to work through and close down. It was that simple—that straightforward. Where did all this chasing feature? He was *Rocco Hermida*. He didn't *chase*. Not like this. Not like a stupid adolescent.

If she wanted him the way he knew she wanted him she could damn well quit her coy little act and juvenile games. She could come and get him. And she would.

He smiled grimly at the passing scenery as he made his way back to Recoleta. Yes, she would. He would lay money on it. His Irish obsession? *Su obsesion Argentina!* *Her* Argentinian obsession. She was right in it with him. Up to her neck.

Frankie pulled closed the curtain as the sleek black car skirted the corner and vanished. She stepped back into the shabby-chic room and sat down on the edge of the bed. In a short silk shift, her arms and legs bare but slick with oil, she looked as good as it got.

Her hair was washed, conditioned and straightened into a sleek, shiny bob. Her face was clear, the dark circles camouflaged by the miracle concealer her company were just about to launch. She had lined her eyelids with shadow the same blue as her dress and coated her lashes in black. Lip gloss plumped her lips and the lightest hint of bronzer dusted her cheeks. She'd come a long, long way from the pony-mad teenager who'd tried to bag Rocco Hermida.

So why had she not quite been able to follow through?

One look at the television screen showing the pictures the rest of the world would be watching—well, the rest of the polo world—had confirmed it all. Rocco, Dante and their teammates. Pictures of the match, of the cup being presented, of the fans in and outside the stadium. Of the women who'd featured past and present on the arm of the Hurricane. A never-ending cornucopia of beautiful blondes. One after another after another.

The TV programme was admittedly more focussed on his love life than on his sporting prowess, but still Frankie had been utterly transfixed by the flow.

And when the final pictures of the piece had showed the team heading off with a troupe of polo groupies to a luxury penthouse in a luxury *barrio* this very evening she had sat down and sighed. *Really?* It was one thing to offer yourself on a plate to a playboy aged sixteen. It was another thing entirely to do it when you were twenty-six. Especially when she had more than a hunch of what would follow.

He'd unleashed something in her that no other man could. He had barely touched her and she had almost screamed with need. He had kissed her and it had been all she could do not do jump into his arms and wrap herself round him. And when he'd put his hands on her hips and ground them together…

The ten years she had waited had flashed and were gone and she was back in his arms, in his bed, with that first white-hot flame of passion. But all she'd gained in the past four hours was the knowledge that he saw her as unfinished business. Was she really going to let herself become that? An arm-candy statistic? Would it be *her* face that flashed up next? Entering the Molina Lario at his side for the whole world to see? The whole world, including her father...

She had battled her way out of the black fog of depression, had rebuilt herself piece by piece, layer by layer, after her father had stripped her bare of everything she'd ever cared about. Hidden her away and punished her. The bruise of the slap that had landed across her cheek had faded so much faster than the bruise that had bloomed across her heart for all those years.

Was being Rocco's 'Irish squeeze' going to be her legacy? Her mother would have a fit and her father would roll his 'I told you so' eyes.

She lifted up the remote control and changed the channel to some glitzy, ritzy soap opera—probably much like Rocco Hermida's life. And what would *her* part be? The beautiful heroine? Hardly. More like the kooky best friend put in as a comedy foil. Because that was the other thing—she didn't really measure up as his type of leading lady. She was distinctly lacking on all the fronts he seemed to major in—like big hair and big breasts. And, though her confidence was never rock bottom now, it was hardly skyscraper high, either.

A tiny part of her did wonder, even if she arrived at Molina Lario with Rocco, was sure she would leave with him, too? After all, she'd never managed to stay the course with any previous man.

She was twenty-six. She was doing well for herself. She didn't need to create a whole load of heartache. So she'd waited ten years to see if he was still as hot as she remembered? Answer—yes. What was the next question? Was there going to be a day after the morning-after? Answer— no. Conclusion—*put all thoughts of Rocco Hermida out of*

your head. And don't spend the next ten years in the same
state of perpetual wonder as the past ten.

There were bound to be other men who could light
her up like he did. Surely!

Frankie turned the television off altogether and sighed.
Her phone flashed and she leaned across to the bedside
table to check it. Esme.

Hey, beautiful. We need you! Come shake off your jet
lag and meet the Palm Beach boys. Told them all about
you so you'd better get here soon! No excuses! X

She stared at the message. She could pretend she
hadn't seen it. She could turn her phone off and read
her emails instead. But, knowing Esme, she'd turn up
and drag her out anyway. So should she? Meet the Palm
Beach boys? Maybe that would be just the thing to cure
this once and for all. To go. Confront her demon. Let
the dream shatter for good. And maybe she'd even get
herself worked up over some other handsome man who
was just a fraction less arrogant, less dominant, less utterly overwhelming.

The phone lit up again.

The car's on its way. Tango time! X

That was decided, then. She stood up. In her silver
sixties slingbacks she made all of five-five—'the height
of nonsense', as her father had used to say, and not in a
good way. But whatever she was, she was big enough to
play in the playgrounds of the *porteños* and their Palm
Beach buddies.

She could pull this off. Of course she could. If she
could lift herself out of the blackest depression and keep

it at bay for all these years she could damn well paint on a smile, slip in and hang out with her best friend.

Esme knew more than anyone that parties weren't her thing, but this was a watershed moment. A mark of her own maturity. She had weighed it all up and traded a night or an hour with Rocco 'Hurricane' Hermida. She had so much more to get from life than an empty inbox and a roll in his hay.

She slipped on the Bolivian silver earrings she'd bought at a market in the Dominican Republic, grabbed her clutch. Incredible that two days earlier she'd bought these earrings, totally unaware that Rocco Hermida would hurricane his way back into her life. But there was nothing surer that in two days' time, regardless of what happened, he would be hurricaning his way back out of it.

Just remember that, she told her wild side. *Remember that and stand well back.*

CHAPTER THREE

THE GLAMOUR OF polo had never held any attraction for Frankie. Sure, she'd learned how to dress, how to style her hair—okay, she'd learned how to plug in straighteners—and since working at Evaña Cosmetics for the past four years she'd grudgingly warmed to the wonders of make-up.

But the hats and the heels, the sponsorship deals and the general buzz about anything related to the ponies or the players she could still, if she was honest, pass on.

Tonight, though, entering the grand Molina Lario Hotel—a French-style mansion house renowned for its exclusive, excessive entertainments—she lapped up the atmosphere and soaked up the vibe. People there exuded something purposeful, joyful and wholly sensual—and it seemed to chime with the city itself. There was passion in the air and there was anticipation all around. She could smell it. She could taste it. Would it be possible, just for a night, that she could actually live it?

She skipped up the carpeted stairs. Cameras flashed ahead, but none flashed at her. She was a nobody. And that suited her perfectly. She glanced at the anything-goes glamour. This was South America meets Europe. It was relaxed, but it was sexy. It was just how she felt. And for once she felt that she'd actually nailed the look.

She wandered through to a lounge that exuded a quiet buzz. Clutches of people were laughing, sipping and looking around. Glasses of Malbec. Bottles of beer. Canapés of steak; morsels of cured meat. Waitstaff in long white aprons and fabulous smiles.

No sign of Esme, but she was in no rush. She wandered back through to the main reception area. An alluring orb of Lalique glass gifted light to the huge oak table below, heaving under the weight of champagne. Its impressive spread drew her closer. Long-stemmed flutes in columns and rows fizzed and popped with tiny clouds of bubbles—*perfect*. That would be her tipple of choice tonight.

Marketing screens were strategically but discreetly placed all around, and here and there the people who made headlines were positioned in poses, eyes on the cameras and smiles for the crowd. The double-H logo of Hermanos Hermida caught her eye and flipped her stomach. So she was immune to him? She was going to pass on him? Really?

Yes, really.

She wasn't naive enough to think that when she saw him her heart wouldn't leap and her blood wouldn't flame. But she was smart enough to know that these were physical reactions. They would pass. And she was *not* going to be held in thrall by her passion for a playboy. Not with the world looking on. Not with so much to lose and so little to gain.

She sipped at her drink and rubbed at her silver ring. A roar of laughter and energy flooded the hallway. A crowd approached along the red carpet. And there he was.

Tall and dark, the flop of hair his instant brand. Blue shirt, dark trousers and a body that her fingers clawed at themselves to touch. Air and energy thrummed around him. Simmering, menacing, mesmerising. Faces turned awestruck and adoring.

Frankie turned away, clutched at the table and steadied herself.

She'd half expected that he would come for her. Chilled when he didn't, she looked back. He and his brother were surrounded by lights, laughter, a myriad of love. He looked at her—just for a moment. Long enough to let her know that he had seen her and had dismissed her.

Was that it? Had she had her moment in the sun? Had he already moved on?

Of course.

She was ridiculous to think otherwise.

Suddenly her 'New Frankie' plan seemed preposterous. She put down the flute, saw the huge smudge of lip gloss on its edge and rubbed at it almost apologetically. Esme must be here somewhere. She would find her and camp out with the Palm Beach crew. That had been her plan all along, and she owed it to Esme and to herself to follow through. It was either that or go back to the hotel. And, really—was she going to give in *that* easily?

Still aware of the Hermida circus to her left, she turned her back and fumbled in her bag, found her phone. Thank God for distraction. And a text from Esme.

Hurry up! Tango Bar—Hugo waiting. ;-)

There were lots of Hugos in the world of polo, but only one on the Palm Beach team. He was nice, she supposed—a tall, square-jawed picture of health and handsomeness. And he played well—really well. But the thought of small talk with such a big guy held very little appeal.

She clicked off her phone and dropped it back in her bag. Still, if she was going to make a go of the evening, she'd better fill it with something other than the mouth-watering sight of Rocco.

Her eyes slipped away of their own accord, to see if she was even on his radar, but he was now in front of the screens, his arms round some girls, gaze straight ahead. The understated scowl of a smile just added to his allure and made her recoil like a sulky cat. So she was *that* disposable?

Tango music drifted up the stairs, meaning that she was going to have to walk past the impromptu photo-shoot to get to it. She could do that. Sure she could.

Trying to paint 'not bothered' all over her face, she tilted up her chin and began her stalk past. A photographer stepped back to get a better shot and she had to swerve swiftly to avoid him. Her ankle twisted in her shoe and she swallowed a yelp of pain.

Big biceps reached out, steadied her. She looked up, startled, into the face of Dante Hermida. Like a sunbeam of happiness he sorted her stumble, flooded her path with smiles.

'Hey—are you okay?'

His touch was disarming, warming, lingering just that second more than necessary.

Solid—like a brother's.

'Fine. Thanks.'

'Are you sure? You seemed in a bit of a rush, there.'

Frankie opened her mouth to speak, but a figure immediately loomed up, put an arm across Dante's shoulder, steering him round.

'I'll take over here.'

Rocco. Like an unexploded bomb.

His brother didn't lose a beat.

'You reckon?'

Rocco didn't even reply, just exuded danger.

Frankie stared from the bemused smile of Dante to the intense frown of his brother. Like a wall of testosterone. One of them was hard to cope with, but two was ridiculous.

Looking past them was not an option. Rocco's eyes demanded hers. Her heart thundered in her ears. Resolve began to crack and crumble.

She spoke up into the rock-like face. 'Thanks—that's kind of you, but I'm going to meet my friends.'

Dante laughed, thumped Rocco on the back.

'You win some...'

Rocco continued to stare. One second more and she would cave in completely. She had to go. She dragged her eyes back and, head down, she bolted. Distance was her only hope. Because there was something he did to her that nobody else could do.

He entranced her. Absorbed her. All she could see were those eyes. She could still feel the touch of his lips. Longed for them.

It was frightening just how much.

She rattled down the sweep of stairs, glanced back— couldn't not. He was staring down. In the sea of people his eyes were trained on hers.

She kept going. Another close encounter? Another lucky escape? Why did it feel as if the hunt was on—that it was only a matter of time?

The Tango Bar was dark and the caress of the music was mesmerising. Simple piano melodies and the undercurrents of slow-burning passion thrummed through the room. She scanned the shadowy space for Esme and within moments had tracked down her party. Another bunch of golden-skinned, smiling sunbeams, not even dusky in the gloom.

Esme was in her element, surrounded by handsome men like cabana boys, and their attention was forced on Frankie as Esme spotted her. Introductions flew past in a good-natured blur and ended with her being set up with Hugo.

Which should work—if she managed to stop her three-sixty swivels, checking who was coming and going from the bar. If she could settle with her champagne and enjoy the company—because it was fun! Everyone was having a good time. Her, too. Damn right she was!

Anyway, Esme wasn't great with no, so she would stay—as long as she didn't pull a muscle forcing this smile—and then slink off back to her adorable little bed. She'd get up for brunch and then catch some sights or work on her presentation before she joined Esme to take the short trip to Punta.

Rocco *who*? He'd be so far in the past by then that she might even need to be prompted to remember him. And that was good. It *was*. What was bad was this unhealthy obsession that had gripped her in the past few hours. It was like being sixteen all over again.

But she was twenty-six. In Argentina. On a business-with-pleasure trip. She was accomplished, confident... *ish* and worldly. She caught herself starting another head twist and forced a redirect onto the dance floor. Surely this next round of dancing with these outrageously sensual dancers would focus her on something other than Rocco Hermida.

She sat on the edge of her small wooden seat, watching Buenos Aires at its best. This passion was what she'd felt all evening. *This* was why this city was alive as no other. Lingering looks, perfect posture, movements laced with stark innuendo. The trail of the male dancers' hands over their partners and the mirrored responses. Truly, she was spellbound.

When the first round of tunes had passed a dancer approached her, and she rose as if in a trance to join him on the floor. Esme whooped behind her and she suddenly wondered how she'd got to the edge of the floor, in the light grasp of this man, when she was pretty likely to make a fool of herself.

Those dreaded Saturday-morning dance lessons might turn out to be useful after all. Six months of her life, dragged there by her mother, who'd been worried she would turn into a boy completely.

There had been no way Frankie would signed up for the local Irish-dancing classes, for fear any of her classmates would see her. But she had reluctantly agreed to a block of ballroom lessons, which everyone had found strange at the time. Strange—but no one had complained. And she might have kept it up—it had been quite fun— but her Saturday mornings had been precious. They'd been for ponies and stick-and-ball practice. So, age fourteen, she'd put her foot down and refused to return. Stubborn, she supposed. At least that what everyone had said she was.

And proud.

So she kept her head up now and moved in the way he directed, basic steps coming back to her moment by moment. She'd been so charged since she'd arrived in this city she felt as if she must be oozing passion, and this dance was just what she needed to get some of it out. She stepped as he stepped and turned when he threw her, spilled herself back into his arms.

Right back. Right in front of Rocco.

There, at another small table at the side of the floor,

he was sitting. Watching. One arm over the back of the
chair, strong legs splayed open. Face in a scowl of such
intensity. He stared right into her eyes. She felt her legs
almost buckle. But she was scooped up and she finished
the dance. Clearly a novice, but she hadn't disgraced herself. Except for that moment.

The music stopped. A kiss of her hand and she was
escorted back to her seat. Everyone whooped at her bra-
vado, high-fived her first-timer success, and she sat
flushed and alive and breathless.

And then he was up. On his feet. Walking onto the
floor. Walking around a female dancer. Stirring up the
crowd. As the melody started, the place buzzed and bub-
bled expectantly.

'He dances as he plays,' she heard Hugo say. 'And
he used to box. Lightning reflexes—fearless and utterly
controlled. What a guy.'

He was everyone's hero.

His partner—blond hair slick and tied at the nape
of her neck, short red low-cut dress, nude high heels—
dipped her eyes and her head and answered his sensual
commands. Wound her body slowly with his, stepped
in quicksilver paces and flicked lightning-fast kicks.
Rubbed her hands all over him. And he stood there. Di-
recting her. Absorbing her. Tall, straight, thoroughbred
man. They were electrifying.

Frankie's heart pulsed. It was too much. Too much to
bear. She shoved herself up from the table and pushed
her way out through the crowd. Hating her stupid, ridiculous reaction to watching this man! He was just a man!
So why had she given him this power over her?

She raged as she made her way upstairs and along a
dimly lit porticoed hallway to the ladies' room. A five-
minute break and she'd go back to Esme, tell her she was

done for the night, and then head off to her bed. It was still only 2:00 a.m., and they'd all be out for hours, but she'd had enough. She would work on her presentation tomorrow, meet up with Esme and then head for Punta. Then her last trip out to the Pampas and then back to Madrid. She couldn't wait.

She brushed her hair, reapplied lip gloss and scowled at herself. Enough was enough. She was back in the game. Time to take control properly. Today could be chalked up to a bad trip down memory lane, but it ended here. Now.

She pushed the doors open to go and let Hugo down gently and bid Esme good-night.

But one step out into the quiet corridor and her arm was tugged, her hand clasped and off she was dragged. Rocco took four strides and turned into a dark alcove. He hauled her round and threw her down onto a hard velvet love seat as if he was still choreographing a dance. She fell down and her head fell back.

'Is *this* what you want, Frankie? You tease me, stand me up—then flaunt yourself all around this party—dancing like an orgasm is waiting to explode from your body! And you think I'll just stand back and watch?'

She gripped the sides of the seat and faced him. Her dress had ridden up and her bare legs skittered out in front of her. She breathed and fumed through angry teeth and stared up at his furious face, still working out what had just happened.

'I thought more of you than that. All these years I have respected your memory. I never had you pegged as a little tease.'

She saw her own hand flying out in front of her to slap him. But he grabbed it and hauled her to her feet. The love seat dug into the backs of her legs. His body was flush with her front. His fury was too close, too real.

His hand still circled her forearm and she tugged it free. 'Let go of me! Let me *go*. Go and dance with your blonde. I don't want anything to do with you—I don't want my name associated with you!'

He fumed, dipped his head closer to her. All she could see were glittering black eyes.

'So that's it? You want my body and my bed but you don't want anyone to know? You're still trying to play the good girl? Even though it's obvious to anyone here tonight that you are desperate for my touch.'

As he spoke he trailed one featherlight finger over her cheek. She shuddered. Feverish.

He drew his head back an inch and smiled like the devil.

'Desperada,' he whispered.

Then he reached behind her and squeezed her backside, pulling her into furious contact with his pelvis again.

She opened her mouth, but the raging defence she'd intended to spit out died in her throat. There was no defence. She burned for him. She ached for him. She had to have him or she would never, ever be complete.

She reached for his face. Grabbed hold of his head in her hands and pulled it down—pulled down that mouth she had dreamed of and kissed it.

She thought she might drown.

Her fingers threaded and gripped his hair. His cheekbones pressed into her palms. Hot wet lips pushed against hers. His tongue darted into her mouth and her legs gave way. He licked and suckled and smoothed his tongue over hers.

He grabbed her head with one hand and the cheeks of her backside with the other. He pulled her flush against him. Hard against him. She moaned his name and he silenced the sound. He breathed her in and she breathed him. Her hands flew around, grabbing hair and shirt and skin. She moaned again and again. His mouth was on her throat, kissing and biting, and then moving back to her lips. She snaked her leg round his waist, heaved herself up as close as she could.

He walked them two paces, then slammed her against the wall.

'You little wildcat. You crazy little wildcat.'

They were the first words he'd said, his breath in her ear as he held her against the wall with his body and ran his hands over her, up and under her dress. He found her panties and tugged them to the side, slicked fingers across her soaked, swollen flesh. The bullet of pleasure careered to her core and she bucked. Once, twice.

'Rocco...' she cried into his shoulder.

'Here? In this hallway? We wait ten years and it is to be *here*?'

He barely touched her and she cried out again—almost a scream.

Over his shoulder she saw a figure, but she didn't care.

He must have sensed it, for he immediately slid her to the ground and sorted out her dress. She stood like a rag doll. He tilted up her chin, smoothed her hair, looked at her with eyes blazing and glinting and fierce.

Then he cupped her face and bent down for a kiss. Slower, softer, but still a kiss that killed her. He tilted his brow to rest it on hers and held her close in his arms. She felt the heat, the strength, the fire of this man all around her.

'I want you so badly. I want you like I've never wanted any other woman. *Ever.*'

He pushed back from her, still holding her head, stayed nose to nose with her.

'You are with me now. The games are over.'

He kissed her again, fiercely branded her mouth with his tongue. Then he stepped back, ran one hand through his hair and took her hand in the other.

'Come. We will go to my home.'

She started to move in a passionate trance, her legs and her head swimming and weak.

'Wait—I need to tell Esme. I'm with her.'

'Brett Thompson's wife? I told her already. I told her you were leaving with me. Told her *and* Hugo. As if I would let you spend another moment with *him*.'

She processed that. 'You did what? When did you do that?'

He looked down the hallway, tension and command rolling off him. 'You'd left your table. I asked where you had gone. They presumed to the restrooms, so I told them you wouldn't be returning—we had unfinished business.'

She stalled and her eyes flew open.

'You said *that*?'

'What? Was there really going to be another outcome, *querida*? Did I force your tongue into my mouth and your legs around my waist?'

Without waiting for an answer, he led her off down the plush carpet of the hall.

Oil-painted bowls of fruit and soft amber lamps lined their path. At the end, the giant Lalique chandelier marked the entrance and the exit. The table below it was cleared of champagne, its gleaming oak surface smoothly and proudly uncluttered. A few people still milled around. More rested in armchairs, their voices lower, softer, tired.

And outside the night was turning to day and the day was only beginning.

CHAPTER FOUR

ROCCO HAD THREE HOUSES and one boat. His town house in Recoleta was mere streets away. They could walk it. His estancia, La Colorada, was two hours away by car. His seafront villa in Punta del Este was a short helicopter trip away. And his boat was somewhere off the coast of Cayman.

His head rolled options like dice as he palmed the small of Frankie's back and escorted her out.

He wanted unrestricted, uninterrupted access and time with this woman. He deserved it—he needed it. And so did she.

He glanced at her and she turned big hazel eyes up to him. He put his arm round her shoulders and squeezed her into his side. She reached up and touched his chest, scraped her fingers across the new wound that throbbed under his shirt. Better than any physio, she would be the ultimate remedy for every last thumping bruise and cut from today's match.

'How long until you go back to Europe?'

He nodded to the doorman and walked her down the carpeted steps. His car rolled into view. He checked each way and across the street. Nobody. He checked behind them. Clear. He always checked. He was always his own security, but he was hers, too—for now.

'A week. We go to Punta del Este later today—Esme and Brett and me. Then I have a business trip to the Pampas on Thursday. Flying back on Friday.'

So she was heading to Punta, too?

'They'll be going to the Turlington Club party,' he said, almost to himself. So was he. He never missed it.

But if the world was heading to Punta, he would be heading in the opposite direction. With Frankie.

'I'll take you to Punta. Tomorrow.'

Dice rolled. Decision made.

She stopped right there on the pavement, a flare of anger replacing the passion that had flooded her body. 'I told you my plans. There's no way I'm changing them.'

'No? You've already changed them. You're here now. Are you really saying that you'd rather lie on a beach with your friend than climb into bed with me?'

He trailed a thumb across her jaw as her mouth pursed, framed a retort, then slid into a sexy smirk.

She dipped her eyes, then fired him a look. 'I'll give you a day of my time. After that I'm back on plan.'

He couldn't help but smile back. He didn't normally deal well with independence—women were all about love, not combat. But for the few hours they were going to have together, it wasn't going to be a deal-breaker. So far it had even added to her allure. *So far...*

He kept his hand on her jaw.

'I'll take your kind offer of a day.'

He stepped a little closer to her, gripped her chin a little more firmly and watched as she dragged a breath in through bared teeth.

'And since that's all you're offering, we're not going to waste a moment. I've got a place round the corner...'

His eyes dropped to her mouth. Wet lips.

'If you behave yourself I'll take you to your friends

so you're…"back on plan". Does that meet with your approval?'

Her narrowed eyes signalled that she knew he was mocking her.

'It does.'

'Excellent. Our first compromise. We'll head straight to my town house, then.'

He held open the car door and waited. She fired him a look that told him he'd only won the first round. Then she slid inside. He scanned the street again and joined her.

The moment he closed the door they slammed together across the leather.

Seconds later and the flames roared around them. A pyre of passion.

But she hauled herself back, splayed her hands on his thighs and looked up, straight into his eyes.

'Just for the record, I wasn't playing games. I went to the party because I didn't want to let Esme down—not to flaunt myself in front of you. If it hadn't been for her I'd still be tucked up in my bed. So consider yourself lucky.'

Still in combat.

He grabbed her bare arms, his fingers closing round them easily. He stifled a chuckle. Nodded seriously. 'Oh, I do—I do.'

But suddenly he was struck by just how close they'd come—how far they'd journeyed. How easily they could have lost this opportunity. How hard he needed to pursue her just to scratch this itch.

He added quietly, 'I think there's more than luck at work here. It was always going to end this way with us.'

The car moved slowly; the darkness loomed. Her heaving breaths answered him. Her skin looked silvery smooth, each slim arm still braced on his thighs. She was mesmerising.

He grabbed a handful of silky hair and tugged her head back. He wanted to savour every second, to devour her, to linger over every moment like an eight-course, wine-matched gourmet meal—to swallow her whole.

He met her mouth as she reached for his—succulent as watermelon, sweeter than syrup.

He tasted. Lost himself. Scooped her like sauce onto his lap and let her soak against him.

He sat back as she straddled him…as they went up in flames again.

Seconds more and the car turned a corner, then stopped. They were here.

He reached for the door handle, caught the flash of the driver's eyes in the mirror, held her as he stepped out of the car and strode to the iron gates.

Still dark, the straight path to the curved, domed entrance was softly illuminated with studs of light. His finest home. His proudest purchase. Every step proof of how far he had come from thieving street child to national hero. Normally he lingered, savoured. But not tonight. Tonight he marched with his treasure. Past the low sweet-scented bushes, the spiky-headed lavender and geometric box hedge. None of that mattered.

He had waited for her. And now she was here. Right here in his city, in his house, in his arms.

The heavy half-glazed door reflected them as they stepped up. She looked tiny, slight, and for a moment he remembered the girl she had been. So full of energy, so bold and uncompromising. She might have grown up, filled out slightly, but under her subtle make-up and silky hair and the well-cut dress, she was still that refreshingly natural, honest creature he'd first laid eyes on in that muddy lane.

And finally he was going to take her in the way he had

longed to take her. He could hardly bear any more heat at his groin right now. He was slightly out of control—he could feel it.

His hand was steady as he pressed the keypad, but that was sheer force of will. The door swung open into the high domed entrance. Lamps glowed like sleepy sentries down the hallway. Palms bent their heads in welcome. Portraits calmly considered them. It was as if the whole house was waiting.

He felt her step in beside him.

'Mother of God, what a place…' she breathed.

She was turning three-sixty, gazing at the glass, the gilt, the marble, the grand sweep of carpeted stairs. But the normal flush of pride, the pause and then the proud history lesson, didn't ease from his lips.

'Upstairs,' he said.

He caught her as she turned back to him, hoisted her weightless body into his arms and strode to the stairs.

'Oh, yes,' she said.

She didn't lie back—not Frankie. She grabbed his head, tried to kiss him.

It was the sheer force of the habit of climbing those stairs that got him to the top without missing a step. She was insatiable. He could hardly contain her as she slid her legs round his waist, held on to his head and licked and tongued her way across his face.

He had to stop—couldn't take another step with this erotic creature writhing all over him. He had to take her *now*. Here in the hall.

In a heartbeat he'd scooped his arm up her spine, bent her backwards and laid her straight down on the floor. Her eyes flew open with the speed of his move, but the wicked flash of joy told him she was even more fired up.

'You don't want to take this slowly, do you, *querida*? You haven't got the patience.'

'You can go slow with your blondes.'

She blew in his ear, her hot breath sending him into a fury of desire for her.

'But I haven't got all day, so get a move on.'

He braced himself just to look at her. No one spoke to him like this—*no one*. He would never tolerate any mention of previous partners, never entertain censorious comments. But she did it. And he was loving it.

'You think…?'

She lay still. Just for a moment. Her hair was a spill of the darkest rum, her eyes diamond black in the hollows of her satin-skinned face. Mesmerising. Absorbing. So beautiful.

Something hovered between them in that second. Heavy, humid, portentous.

And then, like a tide taken at the flood, they grabbed for each other.

She pulled at his shirt—fingers grabbing, nails scratching. Vaguely aware of his wound throbbing, he filled his hands with her. Hauled her dress up and over her hips. She tried to scrabble towards him, to get at more of his clothes, but he had to see her and touch her. *Had* to.

He pinned her to the ground with his hand and stared at her slender bones, at the tiny triangle of her panties. She was so delicate, so feminine… Another jolt of lust made him even thicker. Even harder. He grabbed the fine fabric that covered her in his fist and tugged. She yelped and breathed out hard. But she still clambered to clutch at him as he balled the shredded silk and tossed it aside.

'I *liked* those,' she said.

'You put them on knowing I'd take them off. Didn't you?'

'You're so hot for yourself—aren't you, Hurricane?'

He grinned at her again—couldn't help it. She fired him up to be a little more rough, a little more bold.

'I'm hot for *you*.'

He pulled her dress right up to her waist, exposed her nakedness to his hungry eyes.

'You're perfect.'

She was. Exquisite. The neat V of dark hair drew his gaze, and as the words left his lips he parted her flesh and slid his fingers home.

Like a wild beast calmed, she stilled, threw back her head, closed her eyes and moaned. She was swollen and soaked. Just as he'd known she would be. As he'd always remembered. Her clitoris was engorged, begging for his touch, and he circled and slid his finger over it just once. Her cry echoed off the walls and went straight to his heart.

'I've got to taste you, *hermosa*.'

Hands to her hips, he slid her swiftly up the silk rug. She hauled at her dress, dragged it over her head and unhooked her bra. She lay back in the moonlight, clothes cast around under the domed ceiling. She was some bewitching fairy or nymph, clouding his head. Entrancing him. Robbing him of sense.

He lifted her hips, held her open under his gaze, drinking in the moonlit sight of her that he'd never had a chance to see properly in those few stolen minutes years ago. Then he bent his head until his lips and tongue lay between her splayed legs. And then he lapped her, tasted her and relished her.

She had orgasmed in seconds that first time. Caught him completely by surprise. And herself. He doubted she had even known what had happened. He'd catapulted himself out of bed in shock.

But this time as her legs tensed, her arms gripped his

and she burst apart, pulsed and jerked in his mouth. As her cries echoed in the hallway he held her in place and licked at her until she thrashed her arms and legs and begged him to stop.

'Rocco—Rocco, please!'

The words rang out, almost dragging him out of his frenzy. And then he was lifting her, hugging her up, plastered against his body, striding along the hallway, taking them both to his suite. She hung her head on his shoulder, lay limply in his arms.

'Is that what it takes to calm you, Frankie? I must remember that…'

She felt so soft in his arms, lying back quietly as he paced past closed doors. Light was beginning to flood in through the huge stained glass window that marked the end of the hallway and the door to his suite.

'I'm only taking a moment…' She smiled, then tipped up her face, softened by dawn's golden light.

God, she was even more beautiful like this. He didn't think he could wait another second to have her.

He kicked open the door. Three paces and he laid her down on his bed. She leaned up on her elbows, completely naked. He zoned in on her tiny curved breasts, pink nipples erect and inviting. His hands fumbled like a teenager with his belt, his fly, his shirt buttons.

Her chest heaved up and down with hard, shallow breaths, then she kneeled up and grabbed at his shirt, hauled at it. Kissed him.

'Back in the game—*Hurricane*.'

Sweat beaded between them—he didn't know from whom. They made noises…breathed and gasped and murmured each other's names. She was licking at his nipples, her fine little fingers running over his flesh, tracing the fresh scar that had begun to bleed.

'Oh, my God—did I do that? I'm *sorry*.'

He kicked off the last of his clothes, pulled a handful of condoms from the drawer and scattered them on the bed.

'Doesn't matter. Come here. Lie down.'

He grabbed her by the wrists and held her as he kneed her legs apart and then tipped her down.

She strained, held herself taut as he positioned her. Her eyes were on him. His erection. He was so swollen it stood proud, huge, and just the sight of her staring made him nearly lose his grip.

'Rocco, my God…my God.'

She leaned up, licked her wet lips and raised her eyes to his. He felt like a god. *She* did that to him.

His fingers peeled a condom packet apart and she reached to take the condom out. Then she cupped his straining sac and began to roll it delicately. Too delicately.

He'd had enough. His control was shot. He couldn't wait any more.

He shook his head. 'Lie back. Let me do this, Frankie. Come on, *hermosa*. Come *on*.'

She did as she was told. But her eyes drank him in. Every part of him.

Finally he was just where he wanted to be, leaning over her as he'd wanted, as he'd imagined. Finally he was getting to hold her under him and nudge the tip of his shaft inch by inch into her hot, sweet heaven.

She was so slight, so slender. But so ready. And even if he'd had an ounce of self-control left—even if he'd wanted to take it slowly—she had other plans. She slid down to meet him, her eyes never leaving his even as her body took him in and her hands smoothed their way around to his backside.

And he slid home.

The strain not to take her hard and fast nearly broke him, but he lifted her hips and took it as slowly as he could. He felt her fingers frame his face…looked down, opened his eyes. She was staring with those huge eyes, deep and dark and so full of secrets. She licked her lips and drove him on with her hips. Her breasts jiggled as he thrust into her and he knew then that this was the most erotic experience of his life.

'Rocco, baby, this is too good…too good.'

She squeezed her hips even more, and just the perfect tilt of them sliding together nearly killed him. She called out to the day-brightened room as she lost it. He was losing it with her. This was it. The wait was over.

He grabbed her wrists with one hand and pinned them above her head, held her down. Then he threw each of her legs round his waist and hauled her by her hips as close as he could get her. She curled back on the bed, for once his supplicant, and he leaned over her, stared into her and ground himself free.

Released.

It was immense.

He came and didn't stop coming. And she was there, squeezing him home.

Cradling her in his arms, he rolled over and spread her like silk over his body while he crashed back down to earth. His heart hammered and his vision struggled to return. The edges and curves of the white plaster cornice slowly took shape around the dark grey ceiling high above him. The blackout blinds were high on the windows, letting in the morning's brightness.

It was days since he'd been here. Weeks, maybe even months since he'd had a woman here. And he'd never, ever had a girl like Frankie here. Anywhere. *Ever*.

He squeezed her to his chest, almost as if checking she was real.

'What do you think? Worth the wait?' he said finally.

She lay still. 'I hate to burst your bubble, but I think it might need to be the best out of three.'

He smiled. *Trust her...*

She smoothed her hands over his chest, pressed her fingers into the bruise that now bloomed like a map of the world over his right pec.

'Is that sore? Am I hurting you?'

He snatched at her skinny little wrist as she fired him one of her wicked grins.

'The purple skin and burst stitches don't give you a clue?'

She batted her eyes and lowered her head. Kissed the bruised flesh—little whispers of touch with that fiery mouth.

'Is that better?'

He threaded his fingers through her hair, caught them up in a tangle and worked it free.

'I'll live. Come here.'

He wanted to feel her close against him. He was acting out of character, but having her wrapped over him felt so damn good. He loved women—of course he did—but he knew the chemistry, the bonding, the whole emotional fallout attached to the aftermath of lovemaking could lead to expectations he was never going to fulfil. But this moment he had waited for. And he was going to savour it.

'Makes a change from the last time, when you tried to kick me out of bed.'

'At least one of us had our head screwed on.'

He leaned up on his elbow to look at the sleek cat that lay across him.

'You know how crazy that was? You tested me to the

max. I've never been so tempted, and you were—what?—sixteen? Have you *any* idea how wrong that would have been?'

'Didn't feel wrong at the time, though, did it?'

She twisted her head round to look at him, pressed another whisper-kiss to his chest. Nothing about her felt wrong. Then or now.

He shook his head. 'Your family didn't strike me as being the most freethinking. It was a miracle that we weren't caught.'

She turned her head, pulled herself away. Lay back on the bed beside him and stared up at the ceiling.

'We were. Caught. Actually.'

'What? Are you kidding me?'

He shifted up. No way. *No. Way.* He would have known—he would have been called to account. There was no chance her brother would have continued to do business with him—no way their professional or personal relationship could have withstood that type of interference.

She twisted her head. 'Oh, don't worry—I denied it. Until I was hoarse. And Mark doesn't know—at least I think he doesn't. But my dad—let's just say he has suspicions…deep suspicions.'

Damn. He hadn't considered that.

'Angel—I'm sorry. I'd never have left you to handle that on your own had I known. What happened?'

She sighed, and he saw her twist at the silver ring on her finger.

'I don't know. I don't know if we woke him with our noise or if he was just awake anyway. But after you'd got your stuff together and walked out I went to go back to my room and he was there—at the top of the stairs. He asked me outright what the hell I'd been doing.'

He remembered every second of that night. Stifling her cries with his mouth as she came in his hand from those few fevered touches. Pinning her down and then reality crashing round him as he'd realised what the hell had just happened—what the hell he'd been about to do. Trying to get out of bed, pulling on clothes that were icy and damp, buttoning himself up over the erection that wouldn't go down. Heaving on his boots as she'd still tried to tempt him back to bed. Finally grabbing her shoulders and hissing at her to stop, to leave him, she was too young!

But she hadn't given up. Naked, driving him wild. He'd hauled the sheet off the bed and wrapped her up. As he'd yanked the door open and tried to remember which way was out the farmhouse's narrow windows and dark passages had lent him no clue.

Finally he'd stumbled down to the kitchen, past the sheepdogs lying in front of the fire's dying embers, heard the tick of an old clock, heaved on the rusty bolts that had held the door closed.

She'd come down to stand in the doorway to the hall with a haunted look—as if the heart had been ripped out of her. He'd stopped then—aching to go to her, to make her feel better, to take away the hurt, take away his own hurt.

But he'd been young—only twenty-one! He'd spent so long getting to that point, working through his own pain. La Colorada had finally been ready. His polo career had been taking off. He hadn't been able to stay there, to ally himself to a woman—a *girl*. He'd been only just beginning to taste the chance of a sweet future. It would have been madness to go to her.

So he'd turned back to the door, hauled it open and stepped out into the early-morning rain. She'd come right out into the daylight, onto the huge slabbed courtyard, called his name one final time. But he'd just slung his bag onto his shoulder, taken one final look at her, wrapped up like temptation's gift. And then gone.

'He was just standing there—then he went into the guest bedroom, saw you were gone and the state of the room. Saw me in the sheet.'

She turned her face away.

'He slapped me and called me a whore.'

Rocco sat up, but she'd turned onto her side. He scooped her in close, feeling the shock of those words.

'Hermosa, lo siento mucho,' he soothed, furious that he had not known this.

'It's fine,' she said—too brightly. 'I lied. I said you must have left ages earlier. That I'd just pulled the sheet off. I don't know what else I said. I made it up.'

He kissed her shoulder, cursed his stupidity. Of *course* they had been heard. They'd been wild for each other— then and now. And he'd thought they hadn't been. *Stupid.*

'It's not fine. I apologise.' He pulled her back and turned her round, right round, until her head was tucked under his chin. He rocked her, hating the thought of her hurting. 'What did he do? Were you punished?'

She gave a hollow little laugh.

'If you can say being sent away to a convent for two years is punishment, then, yes, I was punished.'

He struggled to get his head around this, but knew he had no small part to play.

'And he made sure that Mark sold Ipanema. That she went to you was coincidence, but it made it all the harder.'

Rocco squeezed his eyes closed, feeling her pain.

'I see. *Now* I see. I didn't think… Angel, I'm sorry. If you'd got in touch I could have sorted it— I could have spoken to him. I wish you'd let me know.'

'You made it quite plain that the last thing you wanted was for me to get in touch, Rocco. Anyway, it's totally in the past—it's fine. I served my time.' She laughed. 'Honestly. It's done.'

He pulled her close. He couldn't deny that. Any more than he could deny how deep the scars of childhood could wound. How hard they were to heal. His own were like welts under his skin. No one could see them, but they were always there—always would be. Despite the 'luxury' of enforced therapy for five years. Five years until he'd learned to say what they wanted to hear: that he *didn't* hold himself responsible, that it *wasn't* his fault his baby brother had died.

Who else was to blame if not him? Who else had dragged him from doorway to doorway, scavenging, begging, stealing and worse? Who else had got caught up with the gangs, the drug runners and the killers?

He glanced past Frankie's scooped silhouette to the tiny battered photo of Lodo that he carried with him and placed at his bedside wherever he was. Precious life snuffed out before he'd even turned four years old. Being responsible for him, letting him down, losing him—it was the hardest lesson he had ever learned. But he had learned it. And he would never ever forget it.

The knowledge that Martinez, Lodo's killer, had never been held to account was like a knife to his ribs every day. But he would make it happen. One day.

He felt Frankie stirring, trailing hot little kisses over him and moaning with hot little sounds. She wriggled against him and he reacted instantly, his mouth seeking hers, his hands cupping her breasts and his knee shifting open her thighs. He positioned himself between her legs, so ready to slip inside her.

'You owe me,' she said as she rolled beneath him, 'and I'm here to collect.'

He smiled as she slid her tongue into his mouth. He owed her, all right, and he was going to pay her what he could. But the guilt that was already unfurling from his stomach was telling him he was never going to give her what she really wanted.

He reached for another condom, turned Lodo's picture face down and held her tight in his arms as he sheathed himself.

So if he wasn't going to give her what she wanted, what the hell kind of game was he playing? Because he knew that with every kiss, every stroke, every whispered word, while she might be calling it payback, he was storing up a whole load of brand-new trouble.

She slipped around him, climbed on top, and his body responded hard and fast again. He might have been able to hold back the tide in her farmhouse but as he slid himself into that gorgeous sweet place he'd been dreaming of for years he felt the world reconfigure.

Trouble?

Totally.

CHAPTER FIVE

HER EYES WERE SUNKEN. Her chin was grazed. Her thighs were weak and sore. Frankie hung on to the porcelain sink and stared at the wreckage.

Making love could do *this* to a person? She'd thought she might be glowing, radiant—rosy cheeked at the very least. The shadows under her eyes looked like a sleep-deprived panda's. Was there any product on earth that could work actual miracles? Not any that she had in her bag. Nothing that Evaña sold could even come close.

She stared round the 'hers' bathroom in this glorious suite. It was easily the prettiest she had ever encountered. Antique silver gilt mirrors dotted the shimmery grey marble walls. Sweet little glass jars held candles and oils, and there were feather-soft white folded towels. Lush palms and filmy drapes. A huge bath like a giant white egg cracked open was set on a platform atop four gilded feet. She pondered filling it, but surely it would take hours?

And how many hours were left in the day? Had she really been in bed for ten of them? A good, convent-educated girl like her? Though in the eyes of her father she was 'just a whore'.

She shivered in the warm humid air at the memory of that slap, those words. The stinging ache on her cheek had been nothing to the pain of Rocco's walking away. And when he'd never come back, when all she'd been left with was a crushing sense of rejection, she'd had no fight left. Her father's furious silence... Her mother's hand-wringing despair... Going to the convent in Dublin had almost come as a relief. *Almost.*

Then finding out that her beautiful Ipanema had been sold...

Mark had come to tell her. She'd been sitting there in her hideous grey pinafore and scratchy-collared blouse in the deathly silent drawing room that was saved for visitors. The smell of outdoors had clung to Mark's clothes—she'd buried her face in his shoulder, scenting what she could, storing it up like treasure.

He thought she'd be happy that the handsome Argentinian she'd been so sweet on—the one who was now scooping polo prize after prize—was Ipanema's new owner. He'd known it would be upsetting, but she had always been going to be sold—surely she'd known that? She was their best, and they needed the money now that Danny had walked out on them and Frankie's school fees were so high. It wasn't as if she was home anymore, riding her every day after school. And Rocco Hermida was easily the best buyer they could hope to find—notoriously good with animals, and miles ahead in equine genetics. Soon there would be more Ipanemas. Wasn't that great?

She'd painted on her smile until he left, knowing that she had nothing now. Not even the smell of fresh air on her clothes.

Dark days had followed. She'd moved listlessly through them. She'd lost her appetite, become even thinner, lost her sparkle, lost her motivation for everything. No one had been able to believe the change in her. Herself least of all. One minute naive, innocent, unworldly. Next moment as if she had been handed the book of life and it had fallen open at the page of unrequited love.

Because it *had* been love. She, in her sixteen-year-old heart, had known it was love. And he didn't love her back. She had laid herself bare, body and soul, and he had played with her a little, then tossed her away.

The only ray of sunshine had been Esme. Relentlessly digging her out of her dark corners—relentless but never interfering. Just like now.

Frankie pulled out a bath towel, shuddered at her own selfishness.

What must Esme be thinking? Her best friend, whom she hadn't seen for years, had been so excited to hear that she was coming all the way from Madrid—had sent a car to collect her, planned to show her such a good time at the Molina Lario, over the weekend in Punta…

She had managed one brief reply to Esme's text to say she was 'Fine! Xxx', and then her phone had been powered off. She cringed, wondering what she must have made of Rocco's dismissive statement that they had 'unfinished business'. It would be news to Esme that they had any business at all!

Frankie Ryan was not a party girl—never mind a one-night stand girl. She was a no-nonsense career girl. A don't-ever-give-them-anything-to-criticise girl. She hated anyone knowing her business, judging her or in any way getting past the wrought iron defences she had spent the past ten years erecting all around her.

Well done, she thought as she stared at her own mess. *Well done for walking straight into the lion's den.* She looked at it—his den. The extravagant opulence. Everything in prime fin-de-siècle glory. Silvery marble and gilded taps, Persian rugs and domed cupolas. And Rocco Hermida…prowling.

She'd walked right in, lain right down and made sure that the whole world knew. So much for wrought iron. Everyone could see right through it.

She'd told him far too much last night. Given too much of herself away. She didn't want this to be a pity party. She wasn't here for his sympathy. She'd never breathed a word about that night to another living soul. Denials to her father, and her mother too shocked even to ask. Mark and Danny both oblivious. Rocco needn't have known.

But it was done now. She couldn't take it back. As long as he didn't think he *owed* her or anything. That would be too much to bear.

She padded to the shower, turned on the jets and jumped back as water blasted from all angles. Then she adjusted the taps, stood determinedly under the slightly too cold spray and scoured herself. You could take the girl out of the convent…

She patted herself dry and swaddled herself in a robe. Used a brand-new toothbrush that made her think of all the other brand-new toothbrushes that would come after she'd gone.

One-night stand.

Whore?

Absolutely not. She was tying up loose ends. She was filing away memories and then moving on. She was here on business and she was having some pleasure. What was so wrong with that? People did it all the time! She just hadn't got round to it until now.

Rocco was an expert at it. Had been from the very first moment she had met him. A roll in the hay and then off down the lane. She was going to learn from that. Surely, if nothing else, she would *learn* from that. Because she'd be damned if she was going to be the one huddled in a sheet with a broken heart this time.

It only took Dante twelve hours to track him down. In person. Rocco was walking back from the kitchen with two bottles of water and a decision about exactly where to eat lunch in his mind. He'd worked up a king-size appetite, and as soon as Frankie came out of the shower he was going to feed her, nourish her, make sure she had enough fuel for them to continue where they'd left off. It was pretty much all he had head space for just now.

He'd done too much thinking in the past few hours—watching her as she slept, biting down on his anger. He should have done more at the time. He should have checked she was all right. He should have at least figured out that the reason she'd never been mentioned was that she'd been sent away in disgrace.

Damn, but this just proved his point. Being responsible for others was a non-negotiable non-starter. Lodo, Dante—and now this. Nothing good came of it but feelings of guilt, regret, that he could have done more.

What concerned him most was that even though she had every right to hate him and hold him responsible she had come here—after all this time. And no matter what she claimed—that it was a business trip, that she'd wanted to see the ponies—she had tracked him down. And right now she was in his bedroom.

That part wasn't the problem—not at all. And she didn't seem like the kind of woman who'd turn needy and emotional. But still, you never knew… Sometimes it was the wild ones who were the most vulnerable.

So he had to be crystal clear that this was a short-term party for two. With no after-party. Of course, that would be a whole lot easier if he wasn't so turned on by her.

If he'd been able to get her out of his system like every other woman before. But that wasn't looking as if it was going to happen any time soon.

'Hey, *guapo*!'

Rocco paused, and scowled at Dante as he sauntered in from the grounds.

'What are *you* doing here?'

Dante's easy golden grin slid over him, for once jarring his mood.

He didn't want to be disturbed—didn't want to have to think through or account for what he was doing. He just wanted to enjoy it while it lasted.

'You didn't seriously think I would stay away? Took me a while to track you down, though. Never thought you'd hole up *here*.'

He drew a hand through his dark blond hair, reached for one of the bottles of water.

'There's more in the fridge. These are for us.'

'*Us*? As in *la chica irlandés*? So she's still here?'

He whistled. And grinned. And removed his hand when he saw that Rocco wasn't going to relinquish the bottle.

'Ah. So we're still working through the obsession?'

He nodded his head. 'We're getting there.'

Dante was smirking, prowling about, checking things out.

'You got plans?' Rocco cracked the lid on his water, necked half of it, tried to swallow his irritation at the same time.

'Well, the party's moved on—everybody's in Punta. Waiting on *you*.' He tossed away his jacket and eased himself onto a sofa, looking as if he was just about to film a commercial. As usual.

'Don't let me hold you back. I've got stuff to do at the estancia. Might take me the weekend to fix—'

Dante ignored him, cut in. 'You know you've created a whole lot of buzz? The way you acted last night. But hey, it's cool. I'll get out of your hair. Leave you to work all the knots out. God knows you've been coiled up with it for years. A whole weekend, though? Impressive.'

'You're reading too much into this.'

'What about Turlington?'

'What about it?'

Dante pulled out his phone, started to browse through it as if he had all the time in the world. That was the thing about Dante—he made easy an art form.

'Oh, nothing. Except you've never missed it yet. And there will be a lot of disappointed people there if you don't show up.' He grinned at his phone. 'In fact there will be a lot of disappointed people if you *do* show up with *la chica*. What's her name again? Frankie?'

'Yeah, that's me.'

They both turned round. And there she was. Framed in falling sunbeams from the hallway, golden all around. She walked towards them into the kitchen. And if he'd thought she'd looked sexy in her little blue dress, it was nothing to seeing her decked out in one of his favourite blue shirts. Scrubbed clean, hair sleek, bare limbs.

Had she done the buttons up wrong just to add to the whole 'tumbled out of bed' look? His eyes zoned straight in on the asymmetric slices of fabric that skimmed her toned, succulent thighs.

She strolled right up and took the bottle of water that was dangling limply from his hand. Then she unscrewed the top, tipped the bottle head against his, winked, said, 'Cheers!' and took a long, slow sip.

His eyes zoned in on her throat. Swallowing the water. It killed him.

He'd really thought that some of her allure would have rubbed off by now. Didn't feel like it. Not the way he was warming up. He turned away.

Dante beamed at her as if she was some kind of clever child who had taken its first steps or said its first words. Then he did exactly what he always did: he stood up and sauntered over as if he was being called to the stage to collect a prize—all easy charm and sunshine smiles.

'I'm Dante. *Absolute* pleasure to meet you, Frankie. Again.'

He kissed her right cheek, kissed her left cheek. Held her by the shoulders and gave her a long once-over. Nodded.

Rocco sank the rest of his water and watched from the corner of his eye.

She was smiling that smile. She could be so intense, but when she smiled her face lit up like *carnival*.

'Pleased to meet you, too, Dante. *Again.*'

'Dante's just leaving.' He took his empty bottle and fired it into the recycling bin. It clattered noisily.

Dante didn't miss a beat.

'Yeah, I'm heading to Punta, Frankie. We always head there after the Molina party. It's the Turlington Club party tomorrow night. I'd be happy to take you.'

It was the usual chat, but seeing the flash of dipped eyes and the curve of a smile made him bristle. Was she flirting? Was Dante flirting right back? Whatever—it was pushing his damn buttons. That was all it was. He should know that. What was *wrong* with him? He should calm the hell down.

She opened her mouth to reply but he cut in. 'As I said,

I have to call in at La Colorada. So I'll let you know later if I'm going to make it up to Punta.'

'How about you, Frankie? What would you rather do? Go and muck out horses with the Lone Ranger here, or drink cocktails at Bikini Beach with me?'

Rocco felt his fingers grip Frankie's shoulders. 'Frankie came all the way here to *see* the horses, so I reckon that answers your question.'

'And I thought she was here to see you...'

The swine threw his head back and laughed. Round One to him.

Rocco palmed her back as he steered her down the hallway, with Dante's chuckling words ringing in the space. 'I'll see myself out, then. See you at the Turlington Club, Frankie—save me a dance.'

How many times had Dante tried that routine on one of his girls? And how many times had Rocco found it entertaining? Countless. Watching their eyes widen, wondering who to look at—wondering if Dante really *was* flirting.

'You never said anything about going to your ranch.'

She had stopped dead, in that way that she did. Like a mule.

'No, I didn't, but I have to go there now.'

He paused. This could be the moment. At any other time, with any other woman, this *would* be the moment. As soon as they got possessive, bitchy or mean: *It's been great, but change of plans. Thanks for a wonderful time.* It would be that clean. The words would maybe sound harsh, but it would be short, sweet, simple.

He considered, but he just didn't want to. Not yet anyway. Another day should see all the knots worked out...

'But I've already told you I was only here with you for the day. I've come halfway across the world to see Esme.'

She was still with *that*? She couldn't see herself that the minute she'd landed it was *him* she'd tracked down? He was still coming to terms with everything she'd told him, but he was slowly getting there—she couldn't really be blind to the fact that it was *his* house she was standing in, in *his* shirt, after having *his* body all over her for the past ten hours.

'Punta is a two-hour trip. If you want to leave now I'll make the arrangements...'

She opened her mouth.

'I have to go to the estancia. Juanchi, my head gaucho, wants to talk. He's got a concern about one of the ponies on the genetics programme. It's up to you. Easy to get you to your friends, if that's what you want.'

She twirled a strand of hair, made a little face, shrugged. 'Okay. Sounds like a plan. As long as there are no more surprises.'

Sounds like a plan? No more surprises? He almost did a double-take. God, she riled him like no other woman ever could.

But even as she stood there he wanted to wipe the coy little look off her face with his mouth.

'That's the thing about surprises—you can't always see them coming.'

She slipped him a little smile. 'I suppose...'

'Take us—right now.'

He took the water from her hand, put it on the console table beside them.

'Bolt from the blue.'

He slid his hands round her waist, felt the faint outline of her ribs, pulled her towards him. She was still holding back. Still playing her game. He could feel it. No arms round his neck...no legs round his waist.

'This has been a very lovely surprise. Gorgeous.'

He stepped into her space, eased his thumbs to the underside of her breasts. Slowly, slowly rubbed the soft flesh, gently massaged.

'So what if it's only going to last a few more hours? A day? You go your way—I go mine.'

He kept up his sensuous caressing. She blinked her eyes, slowly, softened like butter in the sunshine.

'But there's no point denying that right now we're very...'

His hands slid to the sides of her breasts and his thumbs found her nipples. Little light touches to begin with, just how she liked it.

'Very...'

She closed her eyes.

'Hot for one another...'

Her head fell back and she ground out a long, satisfied sigh. 'Mmm...'

He nodded. Slid one hand to the hem of the shirt, gripped her hips, kept up the pressure on her nipples. Then he bent his mouth to the fabric, drew long and deep on each nipple, soaked his own shirt with his mouth, tugging those buds to hard points.

She was so easy to turn up and down, on and off. Like a geyser.

He stood back, admired his work.

'Lose the shirt,' he said.

For a moment she stood, dreamy and drugged. Then she fixed him with a look. Dipped her chin. Smiled like sin.

'Make me.'

He grinned. He couldn't help it. There she went again—matching him. Firing him up. Making him feel that here was a woman who could stand toe to toe with him.

Dammit, but he couldn't afford to let crazy thoughts like those into his head.

He grabbed for her. '*Make* you, Angel? In ways you've never even dreamed of...'

She tried to duck away but he caught her. She screamed with laughter as he hauled her close to him and silenced her with kisses like a crazy man. She caved. Totally caved. Couldn't get enough. She suckled his lip, his tongue, showered him with kisses.

She thought *she* was calling the shots?

He needed to be in complete control of this. Couldn't afford any slip-ups.

He tossed her over his shoulder. Her shirt—*his* shirt—rode up, and he held his hand over her bare backside, bringing it down just a little hard. Just a little warning—*he* was in control. And that was how it would stay.

CHAPTER SIX

FRANKIE WAS PREPARED for the long jacaranda-lined driveway. She was prepared for the still green lakes overhung with sleepy willows. The curved pillared entrance, the endless array of white-framed windows, the pops of colour from plants, pots and baskets—all of them were totally as she'd envisaged. She was even prepared for the unending horizons she could see on either side of the mansion-style ranch house, rolling into the distance, underlining the vastness of the lands, the importance of the estancia, the power of the man.

But she was not prepared for the huge lump that welled in her throat or the hot tears that sprang to her eyes when she saw the horses that galloped over to the fence to welcome their master home, racing alongside the car as he drove, happily displaying their unconditional love. Nor was she prepared for the uninhibited smile that lit up Rocco's face as he watched them.

The freedom they enjoyed shone out as they played in the fields surrounding La Colorada. It had been so long… so, *so* long since she had enjoyed that self-same freedom. After Ipanema had gone she'd never felt the same. She'd barely even sat on a horse—she'd thought she'd grown up, moved on from her teenage fixation with horses, moved on to her adult fixation with escape.

But here, now, it all came flooding back. Maybe it was just because she was so tired, or maybe it was a reflection of all that had come at her these past several hours, but she struggled to hold back a sob as memories of her happy childhood slammed into her one after another after another. A childhood that had been so completely shattered with the arrival of Rocco Hermida.

She twirled her ring and swallowed hard.

'I have to find Juanchi. You can wait in the house—relax until supper. Come on, I'll show you inside.'

Those were the first words he had spoken to her in the best part of an hour. They'd gone back to bed, both drifted off to sleep, and when she'd woken he'd been pulling on clothes with his phone clamped to his ear. It hadn't moved far ever since.

Her little vinyl carry-on case had arrived, its gaudy ribbon, scuffed sides and wonky wheel incongruous beside the butter-soft leather weekend bag Rocco had been chucking things into as he spoke.

Rattling out questions, he'd glanced at her, given a little wink, then turned his back and walked to the window, continuing to berate the poor director of some vineyard who was on the other end. His hand had circled and stabbed at the air as he'd punctuated his questions with a visual display of his frustration.

She'd showered and dressed quickly in what she'd thought might be appropriate—denim shorts and a pink T-shirt. What *else* would you wear to a ranch? She'd slipped her feet into white leather tennis shoes and thrown everything else in her case. Rocco had dressed in jeans and a polo shirt. He'd paced up and down. More gestures, more rattled commands, more reminders that the Hurricane was well named.

She'd looked around, making sure she hadn't forgotten

anything. She wouldn't be back there after all. Spotting her watch on the floor, where she must have thrown it earlier, she'd bent to pick up. Where were her new earrings? She'd glanced all around and then had seen them at the side of the bed, there beside a little photograph. She'd walked round and reached out to scoop them up, but her hand had closed on the tiny frame that lay face down instead. She'd placed it upright.

It had been a picture of a child. She'd lifted it up to have a closer look. A blurry picture of an infant, maybe two or three years old. Bright blond hair, kept long, but definitely a boy. Solemn dark eyes, only just turned to the camera, as if he really hadn't wanted to look. There had been something terribly familiar in the scowling mouth. Dante? She didn't think so.

She'd turned to ask Rocco. He had stopped his artillery fire of instructions for a moment, had been standing framed in the hugely imposing window, an outline of the blue day all around him—so light and bright that she hadn't quite been able to see his features.

She had smiled, held up the picture.

The phone had been dropped to the end of his arm, a voice babbling into the air unheard. He'd paced forward as a thunderous tension had rolled through the room. Something akin to fear had spread out from her stomach at the way he'd moved, the slash of his features and the dark stab of his eyes.

He had taken the photo from her without so much as a glance, but she had felt the wall of his displeasure as if she had run against it, bounced off it and been left scrabbling in the rubble.

Nothing. Not a sound, a word, a look.

He had pulled open a zip in the leather holdall, tucked the photo inside, zipped it back up and then lifted the phone to his ear. He had taken her earrings, dropped them into her hand and then moved back to the window.

The conversation had continued.

She had tried not to be stunned, tried not to be bothered. It was clearly something personal. He was clearly someone intensely private. But it had hurt—of course it had. How much more private and personal could you get than what they had shared these past few hours? She'd opened up to him, told him about her father's fury and her mother's disappointment. He'd told her—*nothing.* Didn't that just underline the fact that she'd served herself up and he'd selected the bits he wanted, then pushed back the platter, folded his napkin and was probably looking around for the next course.

Again.

She had to get smarter. Had to keep herself buoyant. More than anything else she had to make sure the black mood didn't come back.

She'd stuffed her watch and earrings inside her case with her other belongings, rolled it to the door and swatted him away when he'd attempted to lift it. She could look after herself. And then some.

Then the two-hour car journey. The icy silence punctuated by more intense conversations on his phone. Frankie had drifted in and out, picking up snippets about equine genetics and shale gas fields, decisions about publicity opportunities he wanted reversed. *Now.*

She had rummaged in her bag, pulled out a nail file. She'd filed her nails into perfect blunt arcs. The scenery had been flat—green or brown—and the company had been intently and exclusively business. Her phone was still dead and her guilt about not speaking to Esme properly still rankled.

The car had rolled on. She had gazed out of the window, anger and upset still bubbling in her blood. Then she had felt her hand being lifted. She'd looked round sharply. He had smoothed her fingers, squeezed them in his own—the gnarled knuckles and disfigured thumb starkly brown against her paper-pale skin. Still he hadn't looked at her, but he'd lifted them, pressed his lips to them, and she had known then that that was as much of an apology as she was likely to get.

Damn him. Fire and heat. Ice and iron. She shouldn't allow him to win her over as easily as that, but there was something utterly magnetic about this man. She needed to play much more defensively—protect herself as much as she could. Because every time she thought she'd figured this—*them*—out he shifted the goal posts again.

She could have been on a helicopter to Punta right now. He had offered to send her. Not to *take* her, of course—there was the subtle difference. And she had declined. She'd still have plenty of time to catch up with Esme when she got there. Her buying trip to the Pampas was not for days yet. She would make it to Punta tomorrow, the party was tomorrow night—it would be no time at all until this thing burned out between them. No time until she was off doing her own thing again.

If she kept her head it should all work out fine.

There had been more calls, more decisions. She'd sat wrapped in her own thoughts, no room for soft squeezes or stolen kisses. Had closed her eyes and drifted off to sleep, finally opening them as they'd arrived at this heart-stopping ranch.

'It's fine,' she said now, stepping out of the car, and feeling every one of her senses come alive with this place. 'You go and find Juanchi and I'll have a wander.'

For the first time since Dante had left Rocco seemed to look at her properly. He finally tucked his phone away in the pocket of his jeans, flipped his hair back from his eyes and scowled.

'Problem?' she said, with as bored an expression as she could muster. Diplomacy wasn't her biggest skill, and she knew if she really spoke her mind it might not be the best move. Not yet anyway.

'I've been neglecting you.' He looked at her over the roof of the car. 'So much to deal with—my apologies.'

Frankie shrugged. 'You're a busy guy,' she said. 'I really don't want to be in the way.'

He was looking around, as if Juanchi was going to spring out from behind a bush. He looked back. Looked totally distracted.

'I'll catch you up,' she said, walking off, waving her hand.

'Where are you going to go?'

'I'm a big girl,' she called over her shoulder, 'I'm sure I'll find something to occupy myself.'

'Wait by the pool. Round the back. I won't be too long.'

She answered that with another wave and kept walking.

CHAPTER SEVEN

FRANKIE STEPPED TOWARDS the house. Up close it was imposing, presidential. The drive swept before it in a deferential arc. Pillars loomed up, supporting the domed roof of the entrance and the terrace that wrapped itself like a luxury belt all around it.

She could imagine Rocco roaring up in a sports car, braking hard and jumping out, striding up to the doors, owning the whole scene. In fact, she didn't need to imagine it—she'd seen it all before, in that television report of Rocco. This was where he had been photographed with one of his blondes. Carmel Somebody…the one who'd been reported to be 'very close' to him.

She walked towards the door, noted the long, low steps, the waxed furniture and exotic climbers. Frankie stopped. She didn't particularly want to go wandering about in his house—she didn't particularly want to get wrapped up in any more of his life. Not when she was only passing through. Was it really going to help her to have another page in her Hurricane scrapbook? She already had a million different mental images of Rocco: making love, showering, sipping coffee at the breakfast table. She had hoarded more than enough to keep her going for another ten years. What she really needed to

do was start erasing them—one by one. Otherwise…?
Otherwise history was going to repeat itself.

Rocco wasn't looking for a life partner. He was looking for a bed partner and some arm candy. And so was
she.

She turned on her heel. She'd go to the stables. She'd
feel much more at home there.

It was strange how unlike her expectations this part
of the estancia was. She'd grown up with so many stories
of heartless South American animal husbandry. Horses
whipped and starved and punished. But Mark had been
vehement in his defence of Rocco. He had confirmed the
rumours that had rolled through their own stables—of
the Hurricane in the early days, sleeping with his horses
rather than in his own home, spending more time and
money on them than he did anything else. He'd been
notoriously close to his animals, and notoriously distant
with people.

It didn't look as if much had changed.

She picked her way along the side of the house, past
the high-maintenance gardens and round to the even more
highly maintained stables.

They were immaculate. Nothing out of place. All
around grooms—some young, some old, Argentines
and Europeans, men and girls—seemed lazily purposeful. Here and there horses were being walked back and
forth to the ring, or beret-capped gauchos were arriving
back from the fields with five or six ponies in lightly held
reins. No one seemed to notice that she was there, or if
they did they left her well alone.

Rocco was nowhere to be seen.

She walked past high fences, their white-painted wood
starkly perfect against the spread of grass behind. The
sun's heat was losing its hold on the day, but some horses

and dogs still sought shade under the bushes and trees that lined various edges of the fields.

Rounding the corner of a low stable block, she saw him. Off in the distance, deep in conversation with an old, bent man. Juanchi, she supposed.

Even from here he was striking, breathtaking. His stride was so intense, yet it held the effortless grace of a sportsman. Every part of him was in harmony, undercut with power. Everything he did with his body was an art. Kissing, dancing, riding, making love. Being so close to him for these few hours she had learned his ways, his unashamed confidence, control and drive. He was everything she had spent the past ten years expecting him to be. Everything her broken teenage heart had built him up to be. More was the pity.

She stood back, watched, willed herself not to care. So he was Rocco Hermida? *She* was Frankie Ryan. He didn't have the monopoly on everything. She could kiss, she could ride and, now that she'd spent the past fourteen hours with him, she could claim to be quite an accomplished lover, too.

She supposed…

She didn't have much to compare him to—a few disappointing fumbles at university parties, a dreary relationship with a co-worker when she had first arrived in Madrid. But that was because she hadn't known her own body back then. It wasn't because Rocco and only Rocco could light her up with a single touch. Other men could do that—she just hadn't learned to let go yet. Now she would. She was sure.

But even watching him standing on the threshold of his immaculately appointed barn, a structure more at home in a plaza than a field, she couldn't deny he was captivating. He listened to the old man, gave him his full attention, nodded, then pulled the bolt closed on the barn and moved off with him. She watched them walk back out from the shadows cast by the building's sides into bright sunlight.

Respect. That was what he was showing. He respected this old man.

That intrigued her. Of all the qualities she'd seen in him—leadership, confidence, passion, determination, even brotherly affection to Dante—respect hadn't been visible. It showed something about him now, though. It showed that he was even deeper and harder to read than she'd thought.

They turned another corner and vanished from view. Her eye was drawn back to the barn.

Wouldn't it be fabulous if one of Ipanema's ponies was inside? No high-powered polo match to recuperate from, just waiting for a little handful of polo nuts and a hug. Wouldn't it feel fabulous to sit on one of Ipanema's ponies? Wouldn't *that* be worth a phone call back home?

She started across the yard, but the low groan of a helicopter coming in to land made her look to her left. And there, off in the distance, she saw them. All shiny chestnut coats and forelock-to-muzzle white stars. Her face burst into a smile that she could feel reach her ears—she would know them anywhere. Like a homing device, she made her way forward.

They were playing in the field with four other classic caramel Argentinian ponies. For a moment she wondered what it would be like to be able to see them, be with them every day. Hadn't that been her dream job once? What had happened to that girl? So desperate to get away from the choking darkness of depression and the oppressive judgement of her father, she'd moved away from everything else she held dear, too. She barely had any time with her mother or her brother Mark. She was in regular contact with Danny, thousands of miles away in Dubai, but that was probably because they'd recognised in each other the same desperate need to escape.

Two of the ponies noticed her leaning on the fence and began to trot over. She looked about. Maybe the grooms and gauchos were all crowded together inside somewhere, drinking maté, because the whole place seemed to have become deserted.

Would it be too awful to help herself to a saddle? To tack up one of the ponies? To climb on its back and trot a little? What would be the harm in that? It wasn't as if Rocco would even know. It wasn't as if he particularly cared what she was doing. Then or now.

He'd never made the slightest effort to find out anything about her after that night. It was all very easy to say now that he felt terrible, but really—how much effort would it have taken to ask after her while he was negotiating the sale of Ipanema? She'd never blamed him for her getting sent to the convent—she held herself personally responsible for *that*…had made herself personally responsible for everything! And maybe it was that—the tendency to be so hard on herself—that had made her slide so quickly into depression.

Well, not anymore. She would never go back there.

She spotted the tack room and sneaked inside.

Five minutes later she was up and over the wide, white-slatted fence. Five minutes after that she was hoisting herself lightly onto a pony. In a heartbeat she had covered the entire length of the field—just in a walk, then a trot. Then, with a look around her, to make sure there was still nobody caring, she tapped her heels into the sides of the adorable little pony and cantered to the farthest side.

In the distance she could see seas of green and yellow

grass. Brown paths cut through them here and there, and running east to west the blue trail of a stream. Gunmetal clouds had rolled across the sky. And that was it. She was alone, she was as free as a bird and she was loving every last moment.

The pony was a dream—the lightest squeeze with her thighs and it picked up speed, the lightest tug with the reins and it turned or stopped. Most of their horses before Ipanema had been show jumpers rather than polo ponies. Ipanema's grandmother had been a champion show jumper, her mother had carried royalty at Olympia and then Ipanema herself had been spotted as a potential polo pony. When her father had taken her to County Meath she had just won best playing pony at the Gold Cup at Cowdray.

Frankie had been put on horses since she could walk. At age four she'd been able to balance on one leg on the sleepiest pony as it circled the yard—until she'd got yelled at to get down. At age ten Danny had dared her to try fences as high as the ones she had seen at the show trials. Of course she had fallen, tried to hide her broken arm for fear of her father's wrath and then been taken by her long-suffering mother to get it put in plaster. Yes, she'd pushed every boundary growing up—and she was going to push another one now.

Nobody was around. She walked the little pony out of one field and into another. A long clear path lay ahead. She squeezed lightly and started to gallop. On through the pampas, with the seas of green on either side of her as high as the pony's withers. Dust blew up around her, clouding her path, but she trusted the pony and gave her her head.

It all came back—those daily rides with Ipanema, and before her all her other favourites from the yard.

Feeling the warm air whip past her cheeks, the excited thump of her heart and the sensation that she was leaving all her worries behind her, she realised that there was no release like this. No wonder the first thing she'd done after school was to race home, tear off her school uniform and fly to the stables. She'd never known how badly she missed it until now.

The countryside didn't change—just more and more of the same. At one point she was alongside the stream, but then five minutes later it was nowhere to be seen. The huge grey clouds had rolled closer and were underlit with gold from the sinking sun. Sunsets seemed to arrive so much faster here than in Ireland. She'd check the time, but her watch was still stuffed in her case with her earrings… and her hurt at his actions over that photograph.

Who could it have been? Who could have caused such a shut-down? She let the images flit through her mind: the cherubic cheeks, the shock of blond hair. Apart from the scowling mouth there wasn't much of a family resemblance…but then there was no family resemblance between her and Mark. More between her and Danny…

Anyway, she was thousands of miles away from any of them, and every strike of the pony's hooves was taking her farther away from Rocco, too. She needed the space. This was definitely a much better option than hanging around by the pool, waiting for his godlike presence, for him to condescend to speak to her. She needed to get her world back into perspective. She needed to make sure her defences were completely and utterly intact.

She slowed down, picked up the stream again, nosed the pony forward to have a drink. Smoothing her hand down the pony's soft, strong neck, she made a mental note to check out some stables in Madrid. Maybe she should go even further than that. Maybe she should re-evaluate her whole life plan. Did she *really* want to work her way through the ranks of Evaña? Or did she want to go back to her first love: horses? How could she break back into that world? Move back to Ireland? Go work for Mark?

A noise sounded above her, off in the distance. The pony's ears pricked up.

No, she didn't want to keep running. But she didn't want to go back, either. She had put so much into her career already, and had so much more to prove. To the company and to herself. She knew she'd chosen a deliberately hard path, but the payback from every small success was worth a thousand times more than any easy life back in Ireland. Only a few more days and she would get her next big break—or not. It was all to play for—and she was damned sure she was going to give it her all.

She tugged the reins ever so slightly. Time to get going again. Another gallop around and then she'd head back. She was pretty sure she could find her way. If those thunderous-looking clouds hadn't rolled in so quickly she'd have a glimpse of the sun to give her her bearings.

The pony picked up her heels and they started to canter. The noise above her continued to grow. She twisted her head—a helicopter. They were so common here. Like a four-door saloon, everyone seemed to have one. It seemed to circle above her, and then flew away.

She was thirsty—should have taken a drink at the stream herself. She looked around, trying to see where it was. It should be on her right, and if she could find it she could follow its path most of the way back.

A slight sense of unease gripped her. Grasses swayed in the breeze in every direction. The wind was picking up. More low clouds swollen with summer rain had now rolled right overhead, darkening the day and filling the air with warning. There was not a landmark to gift her any sense of where she was or where she should go.

The pony seemed quite content to trot on, but she was beginning to worry that it would trot on forever. Her legs were beginning to chafe on the saddle and a huge wave of tiredness washed over her.

Suddenly, as fat raindrops landed on her legs, her bare arms and then all about her, she thought she saw movement off to her left. She turned the pony round, sure she knew now which way to go.

The rain exploded in sheets of grey. She could barely see a foot in front of her. Her lashes dripped; rain ran down her face. She slid in the saddle and dipped her chin down to try and deflect what she could. She looked around, trying to make sense of her surroundings, but couldn't see anything except wave after wave of summer storm.

She tried to look for shelter—anything, even a tree— but there was nothing except the oceans of grass and rain. Rain didn't fall like this in Ireland. This was vicious, relentless, unforgiving.

Suddenly the pony was frisky. Movement again—and a figure appeared, riding right at her. She pressed her thighs, willed the pony on, but the pony was too excited. And in a heartbeat Frankie realised why.

'What the *hell* are you doing?'

Rocco. Like a freight train through the night he rode right at her. She tried to move away, but he pulled on his reins and spun to a stop at her side. The wildness, the rage on his face stole her breath. She pushed her soaked hair out of her eyes and bit back the shock and the swollen lump in her throat.

'What does it look like I'm doing?'

He jumped down and grabbed her reins.

'Get down.'

'Don't speak to me like that!' she yelled back. 'You're not my damn father.'

The rain was still lashing in sheets around them. She could barely see the planes of his tanned face but his eyes flashed fire through the silvery air.

'For the first time I realise what it must have been like to be your damn father!'

He circled her waist with his arm and heaved her off the horse. Landing against his side, she shoved him away.

'Get your hands off me. Stop treating me like a child.'

Her throat was sore from swallowed emotion, but she would not give him a hint of it.

He moved to reach for her, but then stopped. His hands were clenched into fists at his sides, his jaw was rigid, his mouth a grim slash. But his voice when he spoke was quietly, menacingly calm.

'You caused me to send out a helicopter when a storm was coming in. You caused panic at the estancia. You stole a horse and—'

'I did *not* steal—'

He held his hand up to silence her and she was so taken aback she stopped.

'You *stole*—' he emphasised the word again '—a twenty-thousand-dollar horse. A horse that is part of our genetics programme. Without a thought about anyone but yourself you took off into the country. And *that's* not behaving like a child?'

She heard his words, saw his fury and felt such a wave of shame.

'I didn't mean any harm.'

He stared at her.

'Look at you.' He reached across, roughly cupped the

back of her soaked head, wiped his thumb hard across her cheek. 'Soaked to the skin… Lost…'

She dug her teeth into her lip. She would not cry. *Would not.*

'I wasn't lost. If the storm hadn't come in I would have been fine.'

She could feel the ache between her legs from hours in the saddle, her skin was beginning to chill, and despite herself her teeth began to chatter.

He regarded her with such contempt—as if she was the most infuriating thing he'd ever had to deal with. Then he reached back to his own saddle to a blanket that lay beneath. He yanked it free and held it out.

'Here. You need to get rid of those clothes—for what they're worth.'

She looked at him.

'What? And then you'll wrap me up and make me ride home side-saddle in a blanket? This isn't some damned John Wayne film! I'm not your weak little woman!'

She grabbed the reins out of his hands and tried to climb back on the horse. Immediately she felt his arms around her, spinning her to face him.

'Weak little woman? You're as far from that as it's possible to be. God knows, you might want to try it some time.'

He stared down at her, his fingers gripping her shoulders. She looked into those eyes, at that mouth. She felt the tug of desire and desperately, *desperately* wished that she didn't. She knew that she wanted to slide her arms around his strong neck, wrap herself up in his hard, warm body. How could this physical draw be so strong? So irresistible? But she wouldn't give in—no way, not this time.

She turned her cheek. He tugged at her chin.

'Look at me,' he ordered.

She tensed, but slid her eyes back.

'Look at you? Now? Because it suits you?' She shoved at him. 'But from the moment I woke up at your town house, and then in the car, the last thing you wanted me to do was look at you. Or at your damned photo!'

'I was busy. I have to take care of so many things,' he growled out.

'You're not the only one with a life. With a past.'

He looked away, as if expecting the horses to agree that this was the most exasperating nonsense he'd ever had to endure.

'Frankie—I don't do this with women. I don't explain myself… I don't fight.'

'No? Well, maybe that's the problem. Maybe you should try explaining yourself once in a while!'

She knew she sounded shrewish and shrill. She knew her voice was wobbling with unspilled tears. She knew if she stood another second in his company she would submit to whatever he wanted—just so she could feel that soothing sense of completeness he gave her.

But where would that leave her?

'I'll follow you back to the ranch,' she said to the wind. 'And then I'll make my own way to Punta. Okay? Then you'll not need to look at me, or fight with me, or damn well come and "rescue" me.'

She tried to stuff her wet tennis shoe into the stirrup, tried to hoist herself up. Once, twice, three times she tried, but exhaustion wound through her, heavy and dark as treacle. She laid her arms on the saddle and hung her head, dug deep and tried again.

Then Rocco's arms. Rocco's shoulder.

He pulled her back, and she used the last of her energy to spread her fingers against him and push.

'Frankie, *querida*, stop fighting me.'

He scooped her against his body, his shirt wet but warm. He walked her three paces, holding her close, whispering and soothing. She had nothing left to battle him with, and as he pinned her arms at her side in his embrace she let all her fight go like a dying breath.

'I can't let you go back like this.' He clutched her in one arm and flicked out the blanket with the other. 'I can't stand watching you fighting against me so hard when there's no reason.'

'But there's *every* reason,' she whispered. If she didn't put up a fight now, God only knew where she would end up.

He cupped her face by the jaw and stared down, the angry black flash of his eyes softening as the raindrops suddenly lessened, then stopped, leaving a cooling freshness all around. Light settled.

'There's nothing to be gained. Not when this is what we should be doing.'

He gently brought his mouth down to hers.

Heaven.

Warm presses, soft, then more demanding. She answered him, echoed everything he did—how could she not? His tongue slid into her mouth; his hand slid under her T-shirt. He cupped her damp flesh and shoved her bra to the side. She burned for him. She clutched at him, at every part of him.

This hunger was insatiable. Terrifying. Thundering through her like the summer storm.

He reached into his pocket and pulled out a condom.

'Do I need to carry one everywhere I go now?' he breathed into her. 'What I have to put up with to get what I want…'

And just like that the soft, easy current she was slipping into so easily turned into a dangerous riptide.

She pulled back. 'What?' she whispered. 'What did you just say? What you *have to put up with*? You don't *have* to put up with me. Nobody's forcing you!'

He grabbed her roughly. Shook her shoulders.

'*Why* do you misinterpret everything I say or do? You and I… We are incredible together. And we don't have much time left. If you want to waste it fighting—that's your choice.'

He shook her again, and she felt her world wavering right there. He was right. They had only hours left. Hours she had dreamed of her whole adult life. But she wasn't going to mould herself into the image of the women he was used to. She was who she was.

'Apologise for how you treated me when I held up that photo.' She saw him physically bristle. 'I don't need to know who it is, but I didn't deserve that.'

He eyed her steadily. His eyes held the power and the vastness of the rolling skies above them, but she didn't look away.

'It is…he is…someone very close. Someone who is no longer here.'

She swallowed.

His eyes slid away, then back.

'I see,' she said. It had been all she needed, but hearing the words, she knew she had prised open a box that was kept very, very tightly shut. 'Thank you. I didn't mean to pry.'

She dipped her eyes, but felt his fingers gentle on her chin.

'And I did not mean to hurt you.'

Tenderly he touched his lips to her brow, pulled her against him and tucked her under his head.

The horses stood together, heads twisting, eyes wide. The grasses settled into a silken green wave, the sky cleared of clouds and then darkened and the warm summer day slid slowly into sleep.

They stood together, silent, breathing, thinking, kissing. And Frankie knew that, no matter what happened next, the rest of her life would be marked by this day.

CHAPTER EIGHT

Rocco stared at the phone in his hand as if it was an unexploded bomb. Finally the PI he'd had on his books for the past ten years had uncovered something concrete.

So long. It felt as if he'd been waiting his whole life to hear it. And, no—it wasn't even confirmed—but, hell, it was as close as it had ever been. He'd pursued this last lead tirelessly, feeling in his gut that he was closing in. And to discover that Martinez—Lodo's killer—might have been living for the past ten years in Buenos Aires would be a twist of fate almost too bittersweet to bear.

He'd admit it to no one but Dante, but this news shook him to his core.

He fastened cufflinks and tugged cuffs. Glanced into the mirror and confirmed that his restless mood was reflected all over his face. The shadow from his imperfect nose was cast down his cheek and his scar throbbed—a reminder of every punch he'd ever slung in the boxing ring and on the streets. Every blow, every ounce of rage directed at Chris Martinez for what he had done. And at himself for what he hadn't.

It was the timing of this that was wrong—in the middle of the Vaca Muerta shale gas deal, which was worth billions and his biggest venture yet. That and the delicious distraction of Frankie. But it was too important to let a moment pass.

This was the closing in on a twenty-year chase—one that had started with him running for his life, dragging Lodo along behind him, as the shout had gone up that the gang were back and wanted revenge. And Lodo—trusting, loyal Lodo—had been right there behind him as they'd leaped up from their cardboard box beds and hurled themselves into the pre-dawn streets.

Why he had let him go, let his fingers slip, was the question he could never answer. It was the deathly crow that lived in his chest, flapping its wings against his ribs at the slightest memory of Lodo—a shock of blond curls, the curve of a child's cheek, the taste of *choripan*, the sight of graffiti, the swirl of Milonga music. Every part of BA held a memory, and it was why he would never, ever leave.

Even when that piece of slime Martinez was locked up or dead. Even then. Lodo was still there in those streets. The streets were all he had to remember him by, and nothing would drag him away. At least he understood that now—now that the counsellor's words had sunk in, twenty years after hearing them.

How could someone who was as blessed as he'd turned out to be have fought against it so hard?

He'd been 'saved' by Señor and Señora Hermida as part of their personal quest to 'give back' to BA after they had just managed to escape the big crash that had caused so much devastation to others. Been dragged to their estancia, sent to an elite school with Dante, given every last chance that he would never have had when he'd wound up abandoned, orphaned and nearly killed.

The years of his hating the privilege had taken their toll on his *madre* and *padre*—that was how he referred to his and Dante's parents. They deserved that at least, after tirelessly forgiving him time after time. Bringing him back every time he ran away, channelling his energies into pursuits like boxing and polo that had eventually turned out to be life-saving. They had understood that he couldn't just accept the endless stream of money that could so easily have been his—not that they'd allowed him to squander it. He'd had to work for every peso.

But he'd preferred a much harder path. Starting with only the blood in his veins and the sharp senses he'd been born with. Self-sacrifice, almost self-flagellation, had been way better than any golden-boy opportunities. He had self-funded every step of the way. For him there had been no other way.

And he had done well. Very well. He had everything he could ever want.

Apart from his own family. He would never have that. It was a fruit too sweet. There would be no wife, no child. No one to fill Lodo's place.

But he was a man. He needed a woman. Of course he did. And one who accepted the limitations of her role.

The scent of Frankie wound through from the dressing room. This whole situation had unravelled in a way he had not predicted. He'd thought a passion this hot was just after a ten-year build-up and would be over well within the time he'd allotted. That it was as much about finally sampling forbidden fruit as any genuine full-blown attraction. But he'd been wrong. He was nowhere near sated.

How long it would last was something he was not prepared to commit to—but he was not going to let her out of his sight. Not while she excited him and incited him so much. Pure sex, of course. But sex the likes of which he had never known. And, since all his relationships were effectively based on sex, the currency of this one was totally valid.

Longer term? No. Her expectations would be sky-high. She'd want an equal footing in everything. She'd fight him every step of the way if she felt something wasn't fair. And he had no time for that. He had no time to be looking after a woman like that. That level of responsibility was to be avoided at all costs. Hadn't he proved that? Wasn't his trail of devastation big enough? No. She'd exhaust him. Cause him sleepless nights—in every sense.

That whole episode with her taking the pony and disappearing was evidence enough. His jaw clenched at the rage he'd felt when he'd found her gone. What a fool he'd been. Wandering around the garden first, calling her name, imagining that she'd be lying there waiting—warm and welcoming. Then when he'd realised she wasn't there or anywhere in the house, that sick feeling of panic had begun to build.

He'd felt it countless times with Dante when they were younger—as teenagers out roaming around the city, or later when they'd both go out and Dante would disappear for days, getting lost in some girl. Forcing himself past the terror of losing him had been years in the achieving, but he'd schooled himself. He'd learned. *Dante* was in total control of Dante. Lodo—well, that had been a different matter.

And today he'd been feeling it all over again. Bizarre. He'd been dwelling a lot on Lodo these past few days. Dredging up all the pain again. He had to get hold of himself, though—put the plaster back over his Achilles' heel. And damn fast.

Hours later he was sitting alongside her in the helicopter—watching the raw excitement on her face as the came in to land on the perfect patchwork quilt that made up Punta del Este. The sea, the beach, the clusters of yachts, the million-dollar homes—all were laid out like a beautiful chequered cloth.

He loved this place. Loved that Frankie was here, sharing it with him.

He showed her round his house and the gardens he'd designed himself. Watched her natural interest and joy at the little hidden corners, the sunken nooks, the bridge that spanned the inner courtyard swimming pool—it was a pleasure to see unguarded happiness. He wasn't usually in the business of comparisons, but—again—her lack of artifice, her unedited honesty, was so striking up against some of the other women he'd dated. Refreshing as rain on parched earth. It fed something in him—something he hadn't even known he was hungry for.

And then, of course, there was the passion. As soon as they'd got indoors and he'd got a message that there was further news about Martinez, he'd taken her—fast and hard. Maybe too hard. But she'd responded; she'd given it right back. She was just what he needed right now. No mind games, no manipulation. Just *there*, answering his body with her own. The perfect partner while he worked through this news.

Now he paced to the bathroom door. Opened it. Saw her. Wanted her all over again.

She kept her gaze straight ahead, frowned into the mirror as she smoothed her hair with her fingers and clipped in the emerald earrings he'd had delivered. He would give them to her to keep when she finally left. He would give them to her to remember him by.

The memories he had left her with the first time…

His hands curled into fists as he thought of how badly she had been treated. He had been so oblivious. He was angry, and still coming to terms with seeing a side of her she managed to keep well hidden.

To the world she was wilful, too stubborn. But to him she was just a highly strung filly. As highly strung as Ipanema had been when she'd arrived from Ireland. Missing her farm, her spoiled life. All she'd needed was a bit of careful management and a strong hand. She'd respected that. Needed that.

Just like her mistress.

And now he found himself easily, instinctively handling *her*.

He didn't need to wonder too deeply about why. They were both meeting each other's needs. It was that simple. There was no deeper, darker agenda. It was what it was. And it was good—for now.

'*Perfecto.*'

He said it aloud.

She smiled a self-effacing little half smile. 'Thank you. But I'm not going to lie… The thought of being all over the press as your date is giving me hives.'

He walked to her, wrapped his arms round her as she stood staring into the mirror. He in black, she in white. Her lips were a stain of poppy red, her hair a patent shimmer. In spiked heels, she was just tall enough to tuck her head under his chin completely. He nestled her against him, enjoying the fine-boned feel of her.

'You'll be sensational.'

'I'd rather be a nonentity. Walls need flowers—that's where I prefer to plant myself. And the thought of the media and all those people staring at the photographs of me…'

She shuddered and he held her back from him, stared at her. 'All those people?'

'Well, people who know me. Okay,' she said, pulling away, 'my family. They'll judge. And not in a good way.'

'It's only a party, Frankie. I'm sure they have them in Ireland.'

'Sure they do—but I like to keep my invites on the down-low. It's easier that way.'

'I reckon we can pull off a party without it hitting the headlines.' He hooked his thumb under her chin, tipped it up gently. 'Don't you?'

She rolled her eyes, quirked her lips into a smile. 'I suppose so.'

'Good. So we'll just go for a little while. I may have to return to BA early tomorrow anyway. I have some business that can't be postponed.'

He regarded her carefully, feeling strangely sure that if he opened up to her she would hold his confidence. But, no. That was not an option. Never an option.

'I head out the day after…so that all works out, then.'

Her voice was strained. He understood instantly.

'No, Frankie. I am *not* saying goodbye. Not tomorrow or the day after.'

He held her within his outline, stared at them in the mirror.

'I'd like you to stay on in Buenos Aires—with me. Until…until we put out this fire between us.'

'Rocco—' she started.

He watched her steady herself, watched strain splinter across her face.

'I'm only in South America for a few more days and then I'm flying back to Europe.'

'So stay longer. We *have* to continue this thing that we've started. It would be crazy not to. What do you say? Think about it.'

He didn't want to think about it. He just knew it felt right.

He turned her in his arms. She opened her mouth, as always needing to have her say, but some things needed no discussion. This was one of them.

Careful not to smear her lipstick, he kissed her lightly. But he slid his tongue into her mouth—just as a little reminder that the slightest touch was all it took.

The party was exactly as he'd expected it would be. The elegant country club was bedecked with all sorts of champagne-themed nonsense, and golden fairy lights around the jacarandas that lined the driveway made the blue-flowered trees look like sticks of giant glittery candyfloss. A gold marquee squatted on the lawn at the front of the old colonial-style house that had now become the clubhouse. Grace and glitz cautiously circled each other before the electrifying dance that would come later.

He watched as Frankie warily eyed the obligatory press corps as their car curved round the driveway. He had to smile at how contradictory she could be. So confident, so combative—but also so anxious about being his date.

He smiled, squeezed the hand he'd held throughout the car ride even though his mind had drifted to the next stage of the Martinez investigation—a task he'd entrusted to Dante: one final check on the identity of the man they suspected of being Chris Martinez. He scanned his phone for about the thousandth time in the past hour. Still nothing. He slid it away, held her close, tucked under his shoulder, feeling her presence soften his frayed edges.

Shadows of other times flitted through his mind, startling him. Fleeting moments when the salve of another body had shored up the pain. One happy dark morning, before her breakdown, when he had crawled into the warmth of his *mamá*'s bed after his *papá* had left on the soulless search for work. Feeling her love as she'd closed her arms around him. And then, mere months later, he had been collapsing into the arms of the nuns at the hospital. Hiding in their long black skirts. Racked with the agony of guilt when he'd seen Lodo laid out in the mortuary.

Strange that the touch of a lover had brought of these feelings back. It never had before. The news about Martinez had affected him very deeply, it seemed.

'Here we go, then.'

He smiled. It was unusual for him to have a date who preferred to stay in the background. Refreshingly unusual. He tried to soothe the tension in the brittle grip of her fingers and the jagged cut of her shoulder under his arm as he steered her past the openly intrigued crowd. Fields of happy, curious faces turned towards them like flowers—as if they were the sun, giving light and warmth. To him, Frankie felt colder by the second.

He knew she'd rather be curled up in his lap on the couch, watching TV and making love, than stuck in the media glare with all these gilt-edged sycophants.

Carmel had loved the spotlight. And had stupidly thought she could use her media chums to manipulate him, dropping hints that they were 'getting serious'. Hearing that had sobered him up pronto. *Finalmento*.

And of course Carmel was here tonight—she'd never miss it. All flowing golden hair and shimmering curves in a red sequined dress. Holding court in the middle of the vast foyer. She caught sight of them entering, covered her shock well. But he knew that the extravagant tilt of her head, the slight hitch in her rich syrupy laugh and the twisting pose to showcase her fabulous figure were all for him.

Dante had warned him that Operation: Frankie Who? was well underway. Everyone was desperate to know about the girl who had caused the Hurricane to bail out of the post-match celebrations and go off radar. The fact that she was more shot glass than hourglass, and had never made a social appearance before that anyone could remember, was as baffling as it was irritating for them.

Baffling for him, too, if he was honest. He'd felt physical attraction before. But this was crazy—like a wild pony. Ten years breaking it in, and still it wasn't tamed.

'Look how much of a sensation you're making,' he whispered into her ear, lingering a moment, knowing just how to heat her up.

'The only sensation *I've* got is horror,' she shot back. 'They're like vampires, waiting for blood. Get your garlic ready. And stay close with your pitchfork.'

'Relax…' He smiled and steered her through with a few nods, a few handshakes, but it was clear for all to see that he was lingering with no one but Frankie. He'd need to work hard to ease these particular knots from her shoulders—especially since she was so damn independent in every other aspect of her life.

'Let's get a drink.'

He liked this club—this home away from home. It was old, but not stuffy. The rules were as relaxed as you could hope for, and the people easy.

He and Dante had spent so much of their time here, back in the day. Made fools of themselves, learned to charm, in Dante's case, or in his case, fight a way out of trouble. All in the relative safety of this club that had seen generations of polo-playing Hermidas. Generations who now posed with other serious-eyed teammates or proud glossy ponies, looking down at them from their brass frames in the oak-panelled club rooms. *Full-blood* Hermidas. He never forgot that he was there by invitation only. But he was grateful now—accepting. Indebted.

He led her through the gold-draped dining room, past the billiard room and out to the terrace. Dark, warm air flowed between open French doors and mingled with chatter and laughter and lights. On the lawn the marquee throbbed with a low baseline—incongruously, invitingly.

'Do you want to dance?' he asked, handing her a glass of champagne.

'No. Thanks.' She sipped it, looked around.

'You want some food?' He indicated the abundant buffet.

'Not hungry. Who's the girl in the red dress?' she shot out.

He looked down at Frankie's upturned curious face. So she'd noticed. Predictably, Carmel was on form.

'An ex-girlfriend. Carmel de Souza. She likes the limelight—and you're in it.' He sensed some kind of predatory emotion in Frankie, but for once in his life it didn't make him recoil. 'She once had plans that involved me, but I suspect she has all those bases covered by now. She's never single. *Ever.*'

'That's no surprise—looking as she does.'

'Relax. Looking as she does is a full-time occupation. And I *mean* full-time.'

'Really?' Frankie sounded slightly snippy. 'Doesn't she have a *proper* job? Something with a bit more… substance?'

He shrugged. What *did* she do? Shop? Party? Self-promote? She was her own industry.

'She looks good. She snares rich men.'

'So she's a man hunter? Is that it?'

'More of a husband hunter, to be honest. And with me that was never going to happen. It became a bit of an issue between us.'

She gave a derisory little sniff and he cocked a curious brow. Her eyes, turned up to him, were full of clarity, deserving truth.

'Is that something *you'd* struggle with?' It was as well to know. It had been a deal-breaker before. More than once.

'It's not something I've ever given much thought to.'

He felt his phone vibrate.

'Is that you stating your position, Rocco?'

She'd framed the question carefully, but it would have to wait. He whipped his phone out, saw the screen ablaze with messages and one missed call. Dante.

Dammit.

'What's wrong? Is everything okay?'

'Nothing. Just a call I need to return. Give me a moment.'

He stepped away from her on the terrace, which was glazed with more firefly golden lights. Tried to press Redial. The call wouldn't connect. He pressed again. And again.

He strode along the terrace, checking the phone for a signal. Chatter from the house and music from the marquee clouded the air. Still no connection.

He paced away from the clubhouse, took a flight of stone steps down towards the tennis courts. Nothing.

There was a couple necking in the shadows—he took a path to their left. A gravel walkway narrowed by high hedges studded with flowers, their petals closed in sleep. The trail of party voices was now dimmed, the lights less frequent. Only occasional glimpses of moonlight and his frustratingly inept phone gifted him any real visibility.

He tried one more time.

The phone lit up as a message came through.

Dead end. Sorry. Be with you shortly.

A peal of laughter sounded above the strains of dance music. A breath of wind rose and fell. Around him leafy bushes puffed out like lungs, then sank back. He stood staring at the message.

It couldn't be. He had been so sure. *So sure.* Had felt it so strongly.

He had thrown everything at this. Years of patience. Every favour called in. How much longer was it going to take? How could thugs like Martinez hide their tracks so well? He'd known even as a child that the Martinez brothers were in deep with Mexican drug lords. Why hadn't the police ever caught up with them? Surely not *every* cop was bent? But they'd evaded everyone, and every effort he had put in had hit a dead end.

But they were out there somewhere. And they were not invincible. He was not frightened of them. Not anymore.

He would find him—Chris—the one who had fired the shot.

His day would come.

He stood. Drew in a deep, deep breath. Squared his shoulders. Slipped the phone away again. Looked back at the clubhouse, the party.

Frankie. For a fleeting moment a knot loosened inside him. Like a drop of black molasses slipping from a spoon. Peace. Another strange, unbidden thought.

He banished it. He was getting sentimental—that was all. He needed to get his head clear, keep his focus.

He started back up the path. Dante couldn't be too much longer. He listened for a helicopter, but the wind was rising and the party was beginning to throb as parties did.

He got to the terrace, caught sight of the spill of people all staring inside, through the French doors. Strode inside.

He might have known.

There she was. Carmel and her circus. And pinned in the middle, like a church candle in a blaze of fireworks, was Frankie.

Carmel was working her red dress as only she could. Fabulous breasts up and out, tiny waist twisted, hair tumbling like a waterfall of silk. She would have dwarfed Frankie anyway, but right now she looked just as she had in the bathroom mirror—a pale ghost of who she really was.

She made his heart melt.

'I'm sorry to take so long.' He reached out for her.

'Rocco—darling.'

At the sound of his voice Carmel swirled, pouted her glossy best, offered him her cheek. He had no time for her games. But she was quick.

'I was looking after your date. You left her all alone, baby! Were you looking for *me*?' she added, stage-whisper loud.

Over Carmel's shoulder he caught a glimpse of Frankie's inky eyes trained straight at him.

'Did you get your call made?'

He nodded.

Carmel manoeuvred her way between them. She turned her back on Frankie, rubbed her breasts against him.

'Rocco, baby… Have you missed me?'

She pouted and preened.

A camera flash went off.

She never missed a moment.

He opened his mouth to put her in her place, but Frankie suddenly rounded those sequined hips and stood at his other side, shoulders back and determined little chin tilted.

'*Miss* you? How could *anyone* miss you?'

Cool, understated, but strong. Rocco's eyes drank her in.

Carmel did an uncharacteristic double-take. 'I beg your pardon?'

'Subtlety, honey. Try looking it up.'

Rocco smiled and raised an eyebrow at Carmel. He'd never seen anyone take her on before—never mind trump her.

Frankie slid her arm around his waist, swivelled back to Carmel. 'And, for the record, my *date* has all he needs right here.'

Carmel put her hands on her abundant hips and stuck her head forward, looking for all the world like a turkey in a burlesque show. She started gabbling in Spanish, clearly thinking Frankie wouldn't understand, and she was totally unprepared for the volley that was fired right back at her. Even *he* was surprised at the colour of the words Frankie was using.

'Come. Enough,' he said, putting his arm around her and dragging her outside as she continued to sling one shocking insult after another.

Her feet shuffled to keep up as he quickened his pace, and then he spun her right round, framing them in the French windows.

'Stop, now. *Enough!* Where did you even *learn* those words?'

He held her possessively, and when she still poured

forward mouthfuls of cheek he had no other option. He gripped her jaw and angled her mouth just where he wanted it. Heard the swell of gasps and gossip, saw the flashes of cameras as he lowered his head and kissed her quiet.

She gripped onto his arms, wavered on her tiptoes, until he felt the anger and fight ooze out of her. Fury died in her mouth to be replaced by the soothing heat that only they could build.

He pulled back and smiled at her. 'Finished?'

As her eyes fluttered open there was a lull in the music and he heard the noise of a helicopter's rotors in the distance. He looked up. Dante? He trained his eyes on the lights from its belly as it loomed closer.

What had he found out? Surely they were closer? Surely *someone* knew something about Martinez? He desperately wanted to know the details—still couldn't believe it was completely a dead end—but that would have to wait until they were alone. Right now he owed it to Frankie to soothe her tension and get her well away from Carmel and the rest of this circus.

He led her down through air thick with pulsing music and events that were yet to happen.

'Is there anyone you *won't* take on, *hermosa*?'

He smiled softly at her. She was still tense and tight-lipped, rigid shoulders still not relaxed under his arm.

She shrugged. 'She deserved it.'

He couldn't disagree with that.

'I mean—is it a party in *her* honour? Because that's how she was acting!'

He ran his hand up to her neck, rubbed softly, his fingers bumping against the heavy earrings that even in the gloom caught scattering light.

Suddenly she swung round. 'Are you mad at me?'

He frowned. 'Why would I be mad?'

She swung away. 'I don't know—for running my mouth off? But I can't take those kind of women. Acting as if they've got a mandate on life just because they're every man's fantasy.'

'You believe that? Even if I tell you that some of those curves feel like leather balloons and they're no more real than the those fake emeralds you've got hanging from your ears.'

She fired her hands up to touch them and framed her own face in shock. 'Are you *serious*? I thought these were legit! I've been terrified all night that I'd lose one.'

He laughed out loud. Put his hands on her shoulders, pulled her in and hugged her.

'I love that about you,' he said. 'Of *course* they're real. Totally genuine. Just like you.'

She mock punched his chest and he held her close. There was so much about her that he loved. Even apart from the way she felt in his arms and in his bed. He loved her total lack of artifice—seeing her next to Carmel had been such a startling contrast, suddenly making him see her own Achilles' heel, making him feel so protective of her.

Maybe there was more than sex between them.

Maybe they should talk it through—cards on the table.

Or maybe that would just get her thinking in ways that wouldn't be all that helpful. And he had so much of his own thinking to do now.

He lifted his head to the helicopter that was now thundering closer, recognised it as Dante's. Its lights lit up the lawn, the tennis courts and finally the helipad itself.

'Here comes Dante.'

They stood on the terrace, watched as he jumped out under the copter's whirring blades in a black tux, white shirt and black tie, blond hair slicked back. His movie-star looks were striking. He jogged up, hand raised in greeting, but as he climbed the steps and got closer Rocco saw the usual million-dollar smile was slightly subdued.

Dante glanced to Frankie in acknowledgement and in question.

Rocco shook his head—a warning to say nothing.

Dante nodded. 'Hey! How's the party?' He was an expert, slipping right into charm mode. 'May I say how beautiful you look?'

He took Frankie's hands, scanned her, kissed her cheek. Rocco tried not to care.

'Well said. There's a whole crowd of women in there, waiting for you to say that to them. Starting with Carmel. *We've* got more important things to do.'

Dante looked mildly amused.

'Of course you have. Life just keeps getting in the way, doesn't it?'

'Take it easy in there, handsome.'

'I'll call you. Later.'

They grabbed hands, slapped backs. Then Rocco watched him go. Straight back, easy stride, head high, holding knowledge he burned to know.

Three girls—tiny dresses, long legs—threw up their arms and ran to him. Dante slid them all under his shoulder, not missing a step. Rocco slid his own arms around Frankie, pulled her flush against him. Stood there. Just held her.

Once more the lure of music and dancing and hard-core partying held no interest. He couldn't wait to get himself and his toxic thoughts away—to lose himself in this woman. To mindlessly make love to her until he didn't feel any pain, until he had cleared a path to what he had to do next.

'You want to stay much longer?'

He nodded to the valets and cars crawling slowly by, dropping, parking, leaving.

'I think Dante's got it covered.'

He nodded, tucked her in close again, slid his hand up through the soft skein of her hair.

One thing and one thing only was clear to him now. He was going to tell her that she'd better arrange a leave of absence for a while, because he needed her here. He wanted her in his bed and in his life. He wanted to wake up beside her and come home to her for longer than just this weekend.

And, just like Martinez being held to account, it was non-negotiable.

CHAPTER NINE

NIGHT'S DARK CLOAK lay heavy all around. Frankie woke with a start, for a moment lost, with no dawn-edged window, no lamplit carpet to guide her vision.

She was in a huge space, lightless. Black. Warm. Safe. Rocco's room. Rocco's home.

She flung out her hand. No Rocco.

He liked total darkness when he slept. Blackout blinds, no lamps. Just bodies—naked, entwined—and loving, and snatches of deep, dreamless sleep.

Then daybreak.

But it was still so dark, so vividly velvety black. And his empty space was cold. She clutched her arms around her body and shivered.

Rocco had been more intense than ever in his love-making tonight.

Almost as soon as they had got home he had poured them both large measures of whiskey. His he had thrown down his neck in a single gulp, the stinging heat of the liquor appearing to make no impact on him. He'd seemed to waver over pouring another, glancing sideways at the bottle before putting his glass down carefully. Then he'd cast off his dinner jacket and tie and in two slow strides had hauled her against him.

He had devoured her. It was the only way she could

describe it. It had seemed there wasn't enough of her for him. They'd kissed so fiercely her lip had been cut and he'd tasted her blood. It was only then that he'd stopped his wildness. He'd heaved himself back from her, arms locked and rigid, gripping her and staring at her with shocked concern that he'd hurt her. But she'd felt nothing. Nothing but bereft when he'd pulled himself away.

She'd grabbed his head and pulled him back, and then they'd formed that heaving, writhing mass of fire and passion and pleasure. Hot, slick heaven. No wonder she was shivering now.

She licked her bruised lip and wondered where he was…what time it was.

Her hands groped over the clutter on the table beside her, grabbing for her phone. Her fingers bumped against the glass of water Rocco had placed there for her, trailed over the emerald earrings she'd carefully removed earlier and finally closed around her smartphone.

Instantly it lit the room. 4:00 a.m.

The screen showed two missed calls.

Mark.

Her heart froze. What was wrong? He rarely phoned. He knew she was here. Had something happened to her mother? Her brother? Her father…?

She sat up straight and frowned as her eyes focused, trying to work out the time in Dublin. 10:00 p.m.? She opened her messages and clicked on the link that he'd posted. It took her straight to a news item.

Her brother Danny. In Dubai. A photograph of him walking with a beautiful redhead. So what?

She squinted at the text. *Married*?

The message from Mark was curt. Did she know anything about it? Their mother was in a state of shock.

No wonder! Danny did exactly as he pleased. Without

asking anyone's permission. And the last person, the *very* last person he would confide in was Mark.

Frankie hated the estrangement between them. It had lasted so long. What a waste—what a terrible waste that they'd never got past their bitter feud. She thought of Rocco and Dante and the inseparable bond between them—*her* brothers should be like that. They really should.

She stared at the space where Rocco should be lying. Stared at the untouched glass of water on the table beside it, at his watch beside that, and beside that...

The tiny battered leather-framed photograph of the golden haired cherub. It was gone.

She stared at the space where it should be—where he'd carefully placed it earlier. She'd hardly even dared to look in his direction when he'd sat on the edge of the bed, pulled it from his pocket and set it upright. Almost ritualistic, almost reverential. She'd felt the air seize up, as if some sacred event was happening.

Of course since then she'd run her mind over all sorts of possibilities. It definitely wasn't Dante. He'd been six years old to Rocco's eight when Rocco had been adopted. The child in the photograph was barely two or three. She wasn't given to flights of fancy, but she'd hazard that the child was a blood relative. Maybe they'd been separated through adoption? Maybe that was way off the mark, but there was *something* that ate at him from the inside— something that caused those growling black silences, that haunted glazed look, his overt aggression.

He'd been like that tonight. She'd sensed it. Sensed it in the way he'd lain in bed, holding her after they'd both lost and found themselves in one another.

After he'd poured himself into her she'd felt an instinctive need to hold him, cradle him. But he'd pulled away, closed down. Lain on his back, staring unseeing at the black blanket of air. Lost.

She knew she should encourage him to talk, the way he had encouraged her. She also knew getting past the hellhound that guarded his innermost thoughts would be a Herculean task. But it was the least a friend could do. The least a lover would do.

And that was the dilemma that she was going to have to face. What *was* she to him? What was he to *her*? And even if she worked that out, what future was there for two people who lived thousands of miles apart? He might say he wanted her to stay on, but even if she stayed a few extra days—assuming she could negotiate that with her boss—what was going to happen at the end? How horrible if he suddenly tired of her and she felt she'd overstayed her welcome, like the last guest at a party.

Distance was be the one thing that would give her clarity. Of *course* she wanted to stay on—he was addictive, this life was heavenly—but it was all part of the ten-year fuse that had been lit when they'd first met. And she didn't want to be blown to pieces once it finally exploded. She'd have to have this conversation with him. And before too much longer.

Her phone vibrated in her hand. Another message from Mark…another photograph. This time there was no mistake. Bride and groom. She dragged on the photo to enlarge it. The girl was beautiful, but with Danny that was nothing new. Whoever she was, and whatever she had, she'd hooked him. Danny looked…awestruck.

Wow. She had to show this to Rocco. Had to share her news.

She swung her legs out of bed, reached for a shirt and set off to find him along the cool, tiled hallway. At the far end she could see the eerie green glow from the courtyard pool. On the other side, the TV room was lit up, the flickering glare of the television screen sending lights and shadows dancing.

She took the long way—through the house rather than across the little bridge. The glass walls reflected light and made it hard to see anything.

But what she *did* see wounded her more than any torn lip.

He was sitting on a low couch, facing the screen. The light licked at the naked muscled planes of his body. One arm rested on the armrest of the couch, a whiskey tumbler full of liquor caught in his hand, and the other held something small, square—it had to be the photograph. He was staring at it, unsmiling, as a sitcom she recognised played out on the screen.

Parallel to the room, across the courtyard, separated from him by the illuminated water, the bridge and all that glass, she watched him. He didn't move. Not a single muscle flickered with life. He sat as if cast in marble.

Finally he lifted the glass to his lips and sank a gulp of whiskey.

She didn't need any close-up to see that he was upset. Her heart ached for him.

Through the glass rooms she went until she came alongside the doorway. She stood still.

'Rocco,' she said softly.

He knew she was there. She felt his sigh seep out into the room. He blinked and dipped his head in acknowledgement, then finally lifted his arm in a gesture she knew was an invitation to join him.

She moved, needing no further encouragement, and slid onto the couch, under his arm. He closed it round her and she laid her head on his chest.

His body was warm. He was always warm. She rubbed

her face against him, absorbing him, scenting the faint odour of his soap and his sweat. The powerful fumes from the whiskey.

He lifted the tumbler to his lips and drank. Less than earlier, but still enough for her to hear the harsh gulp in his throat as he swallowed. He put the glass down on the edge of the armrest and sat back, continued to hold her in the silence of the night.

'I woke up. My phone's been going off.'

He took another silent sip.

She spoke into his chest. 'Looks as though Danny got married. In Dubai. Mark sent some pictures that are in the news over there. He says no one had any idea. Mum's in a state.'

'He's a big boy,' said Rocco.

What could she say to that? He was right. There was no way anyone would have hoodwinked Danny. He was far too smart.

'I know, but I kind of wish he'd told us.'

'What difference would it have made? Would you have gone?'

She shrugged her shoulders, incarcerated under his arm.

'I might.'

The silence bled again. He took another sip.

'Are you planning on sharing that whiskey?'

'You want to drink to the happy couple?'

It wasn't a snarl, but it wasn't an invitation to celebrate, either. She pushed up from him but he didn't look at her. His face, trained now on the television screen, was harsh, blank.

She reached out her fingers, gingerly threaded them through his fringe, softly swept it back from his brow.

'I want *you* to be happy, Rocco.'

It was barely audible, but it was honest. Shockingly honest. And when he turned his hurt-hazed eyes to hers she began to realise how much she meant it.

'Come on. Come back to bed,' she said—as much a plea as an order.

She stood, reached for the tumbler, tried to take it out of his hand. And then her eyes fell on the leather-framed photo that he held in his other hand. He turned it then. Turned it round so that the plump-cheeked infant was staring up at him. He looked at it and his bleak, wintry gaze almost felled her. Then he turned it face down, lifted the glass and tipped his head back to drain the dregs.

'Come on, Rocco. Please.'

He held his eyes closed as he breathed in, soul deep, then opened them and stared blankly at the screen.

Frankie turned to see the characters' slapstick antics. They were trying to move a couch up a flight of narrow stairs—a scene she'd seen countless times before and one that always made her laugh. But not this time. Not in the face of all this unnamed pain.

She turned back to see the coal-black eyes trained back on the photograph.

'If you want to talk or tell me anything…? God, Rocco, I hate to see you like this.'

'Go back to bed, then.'

She swallowed that. It was hard. It would be hard hearing it from anyone. But from a man of his strength, his intensity, his power—a man who meant as much to her as he did…

'Not unless you come with me.'

He lifted the empty glass to his lips, sucked air and the few droplets of whiskey that were left. Like a nonchalant cowboy before he went back on the range.

'As much as you tempt me, I don't think that's a good

idea right now,' he said, glancing at the bottle on the bar to one side of the huge television.

She stood right in front of him, deliberately blocking his view of the silently flickering screen and the half bottle of whiskey that was just out of reach.

'Why not, Rocco? Why not talk or make love or even just hold each other?'

He shook his head slightly, made a face. It was as if all his effort was trained into just…*being*.

'Right now I don't trust myself. I don't want to hurt you again.'

'What do you mean, *again*? You didn't mean to hurt me—you got carried away. We *both* got carried away. You've got something carving you up. Rocco. Let me…'

'Just give me space, Frankie.'

She swallowed. He sounded exhausted, but he was brutal. She was brave enough to take him on, though. Him *and* his dark, desperate mood.

She wedged herself between his open legs, hunkered down, rested her arms on the hard, solid length of his thighs. This beautiful man—every inch of him—deserved her care.

'I don't think space is what you need just now.'

She looked up past the black band of his underwear to the golden skin and dark twists of hair, the ripped abs and perfect pecs, the strong male shoulders and neck and the harsh, sensuous slash of his mouth.

She trailed her touch down hard, swollen biceps, followed the path of a proud vein all the way to where his fingers lay around the photograph. Finally she traced her fingertips over his, and held his eyes when they turned to hers.

'What can be so bad? There's nothing that isn't better when it's shared.'

Slowly, boldly, she closed her fingers around the photograph frame.

'Can I see?'

His gaze darkened, his mouth slashed more grimly, but she didn't stop.

Gingerly, she tugged it from his grip. 'Is he your son?'

She had no idea where that came from. But suddenly the thought of an infant Rocco was overwhelming.

'You're opening up something that's best left shut.'

His voice was a shell—a crater in a minefield of unexploded bombs.

She climbed up closer to him, balanced on his thighs. Lifted the photo frame into her hands completely, laid her head against his chest and scrutinised it.

And he let her.

She felt the fight in him ease slightly as he exhaled a long breath.

She sat there waiting. Waiting…

Finally he spoke.

'He's my brother. His name was Lodovico—Lodo. He was three years old when that photo was taken. And he was four years old when he died.'

She held her breath as he said the words.

'I was his only family. Our *papá* had disappeared and Mamá had lost her mind. Nobody else wanted to know.'

His voice drilled out quietly, his chest moved rhythmically and the haunted black eyes of his poor baby brother gazed up.

'I was with him when he died. I didn't cause his death—I was only a child myself. I am not responsible.' The words came out in a strange staccato rush. 'But I *feel* it,' he added harshly, and a curl of his agony wound round her own heart.

She swallowed, shifted her weight, slid to his side and

under his arm. She held the photo in front of them, so they were both looking at it.

'I can say those words over and over and they still mean nothing. I've said them so many times. Meaningless. Of *course* I am responsible.'

'How did he die?'

It seemed baldly awful to say it aloud, but she knew she had hear it. She knew there was worse to come.

'By gunfire. Shot dead. A bullet aimed at *me*. Because *I* was the one running errands for a rival gang. And when the stakes are high, and the police are being paid to look the other way, and mothers have gone mad and fathers can't take the shame of not being able to provide…life is cheap.'

She sat up. He stared ahead. The credits were rolling on the television screen. His face was stone.

'But you just said…you were a child, too… How can you be blamed?'

'How can I *not* be blamed? If I hadn't become little more than a petty criminal—if I had found another way for us to live—if I hadn't got greedy and done more and more daring things…*terrible* things. If I hadn't let go of his fingers when he needed me most…'

His eyes crashed shut and his face squeezed into a mask of agony.

Frankie tugged him to her, desperate for his warm, strong touch as the hurt of his words and in his face gnawed at her resolve.

'What age were you—six? Seven? How could you have prevented *any* of those things happening?'

She stared up at him but he merely turned away, as if he'd heard it all before.

She placed her hands on his cheeks and positioned herself round to face him, held him steady in her grip.

'Rocco. You were a child. And you're *still* tearing yourself up over this?'

His face was a ridge of rock and anger.

She kissed him. She kissed the jutting cheekbone that he turned to her, the wedge of angry jaw, the harshly held crevice of his lips. She felt her tears slide between them and put her lips where they washed down.

'Rocco, baby…you were *not* to blame.'

His eyes were still closed to her but she didn't care. She couldn't stand to see her warrior in such pain. With tiny, soft presses she slowly covered his face with her lips, whispering her heart to him.

He kept himself impassive, cold and distant. He didn't push her away, but she could feel that he wanted to. As with every other time, she let her body guide her, not her head. He needed her. She needed to let him see how much. As instinctively as a flower faced the light, or curled its petals at night, she laid her body around him and soothed him.

And slowly he began to respond to her heat and light. He sighed against her whisper-soft kisses, melted into her cradling arms. He sat back against the couch and she climbed over him, slipped her legs around him to strengthen him, to imbue him with everything she could. The energy and emotion they had shared welled up inside her, and she knew she would gladly gift it all to him to ease his awful pain.

'Frankie…' he breathed into her neck as she lay over him.

His arms that had been lying limply at his sides, not quite rejecting her, now closed around her and held her tightly against him. She found herself rocking slightly, in that age-old movement of reassurance and care.

'You would never do anything to harm an innocent child. *Never.*'

His arms slid closer around her, holding her body and her head clasped against him. He had so much power and strength and yet he was so vulnerable, lying there in her arms.

'I would do anything to turn the clock back. I could have done so much more to protect him.'

'And who was protecting *you*?'

He sighed against her. 'I didn't need protecting. I needed to be reined in. Always have.'

She pulled back and stared at him, cupped her hands around his beautiful, broken face.

'Rocco, don't you even see what you're saying? You were a child, too. And what's even harder to take is that you were trying to be an adult—to make decisions that your parents should have been making for you.'

He recoiled at that, but she didn't stop.

'I can't pretend to understand what you've been through. But I *do* understand that you're adding to the pain of losing Lodo by hating yourself so much for something that wasn't your fault.'

He was still, his eyes level with her chest, not looking at her. The hair of his fringe had fallen down over his scar. She pushed it back and then gently lowered her head to kiss the reddened mark.

'I wish you would leave the hate. There's so much about you to love. Your body is covered in your history— even this crazy little scar. Fighting in the streets when you should have been learning Latin… I *love* it.'

He didn't move a muscle. She moved her lips to the flattened break in the bridge of his nose. Kissed it.

'And this *perfect* imperfect nose. Getting a polo stick in your face because you wouldn't give up…'

She curled downward, holding on tightly, not daring to open her eyes, letting her body guide her, remembering all the things he'd told her about his injuries. The bones in his shoulder were all out of alignment from his falls and fights. She lowered her lips and ran them along each bump and ridge.

Finally she placed her lips over his. Soft, firm, warm. The fires they had lit between them were always glowing, ready to flare into life.

'I love these lips.' She kissed him so softly. 'The pleasure they have given me...'

She felt something inside her contract as she spoke. Waves of emotion rolled and more words formed in her throat. She choked them back and used her mouth to show him how she felt. Softly pressing their mouths together, carefully sculpting and moulding and shaping. The familiar blaze was already taking hold, but this time something bigger, higher, sweeter sang out through the fire.

'Oh, Rocco...' she said as the waves began to break.

He stood up in one smooth movement. She held on as he began to walk, as he repositioned her, cradled her and carried her forward. She held on to the thick column of his neck and pulled herself close as he walked slowly back to the bedroom.

He opened the door and carried her in, walked right over to the bed and laid her down as if she were a silken cloth. He moved over her and stared down at her. She stared back. Up at his face, still intense—always intense—but softer now.

'You sweet, sweet girl,' he said as he slowly unbuttoned the shirt she'd thrown on.

She sat up, threaded her hands through his hair and pulled him down to her. She kissed him. Over and over.

That was all. Just kissed him. Feeling those lips that she'd come to cherish for the pleasure they gave. Kissing and holding and adoring him. Nursing him with her body. And her heart.

Those words welled up in her throat again. But she swallowed them down.

He touched her as if she was treasure, moved her carefully on the bed, began to stoke their sexual love with his mouth and his hands. She climbed higher and higher, beginning to lose track of where she ended and he began.

'Frankie, *carina*...'

He eased her legs open with his thighs and slid inside her. Huge and thick, he filled her completely, perfectly. Inches from her face she felt his warm breath. She ran her hands over the rough stubble of his jaw, felt the enveloping power of his body around her.

She knew the crescendo was coming, but each honeyed beat of the prelude was immense. So perfectly, precisely slowly he eased himself in and out of her. Rocco... her wounded soldier...her love. The words choked her as she kissed him and he kissed her back, murmuring sounds about how he treasured her until she knew she could hold on no longer.

Never, *ever* had she known the depths of such feeling for another human as their lovemaking throbbed to its final conclusion and she broke like a concerto of strings all around him and cried out the blissful joy from her heart.

He collapsed onto her, crushing her, winding her in the most perfect way possible. His hair-roughened limbs and stubbled jaw were her satin sheets. Their breath and sweat mingled. Light from the neglected hall doorway seeped into the room and soothed the night's edges with silvery strokes.

And together they lay, weary, slipping into slumbers and dreams, knowing that they'd crossed some giant divide and there was no longer any way back.

CHAPTER TEN

A WHISKEY HEADACHE was about the last thing Rocco needed as he prowled through the house, drinking water and rewinding the events of the previous night.

What the *hell* had he been thinking? Did he have a body double? What had gotten into him?

The party. And for the first time he could remember wanting to leave the Turlington Club early. Hell, he'd even had to be persuaded to attend in the first place. It had all looked the same—the crowd had been the same, the sponsors had laid on the usual fantastic spread. The only thing that had been different was his head. And Frankie. And those two things were probably connected.

Carmel… Trying so hard to eclipse Frankie and having it backfire so spectacularly. If anything had made him realise how much of a sham his relationship with her had been it had been seeing her beside Frankie, seeing how much of a contrast they were.

Carmel was all about Carmel. She never gave a damn about anyone else. He'd was only ever been there because he'd given her social credit—not because she'd actually loved him… He should have seen through that right at the start instead of being captivated by her body. A body that left him completely cold now. Now his 'type' ran to a whole different set of vitals.

He took another glug of desperately needed water. Dehydrated on top of everything else.

Dante and the news that there was no news. How the hell all this had ended in another blind alley, he still couldn't figure. As soon as Dante got here he'd go through the whole trail piece by piece.

He rubbed at his jaw, rasped his fingers through the stubble. He really needed to shave—he'd probably removed another layer of Frankie's skin this morning.

Frankie. Most of all Frankie. Was he losing control? He was still furious with himself for taking her so fast and hard, hurting her in his selfish need to bury his anger. He'd known he was being rough. They did 'rough' really well. But he'd pushed the limits, and 'rough' definitely didn't mean drawing blood.

And even after that she'd still come to find him. And he had stupidly told her all about Lodo. He felt like knocking his head off the wall to see if there were still any brains in there. When had he ever, *ever* opened up to anyone about his brother? It had taken his therapists five years to get him even to say his name, and he had blurted the whole thing out to *her* in one night!

What kind of crazy was going on with him just now? And how was he going to get back from where they'd ended up last night? Sex that had been tender, beautiful. The best tender and beautiful sex he'd ever had. The *only* tender and beautiful sex he'd ever had.

Dammit again. What was happening? He knew things had changed now. Not permanently—but she was a woman. She'd have expectations. Women *always* had expectations. And *he'd* paved the way for that.

Why was sex such a comfort in his life right now? Couldn't he just rein in his emotions as he had every other time and use sport? Boxing had sorted him out in his early teens, and polo had been his salvation right up until *she'd* walked back into his life.

He really had to get some kind of normal back in place. This just wasn't *him*. Using a woman to help him sift through all the debris in his head showed a lack of judgement.

It wasn't that he didn't trust her to keep the story about Lodo to himself—he did, of course he did. It was just that keeping things tight had worked so well up to now. The closed ranks of himself and Dante were perfect. There was no judging, no explaining. The last thing he wanted to do was *talk* about it. Women were always *talking* about it.

He reached the TV room and saw the whiskey bottle. At least half of it gone. And it hadn't even served its purpose, because he'd sunk it and *still* blabbed when she'd come in—when she'd wheedled it out of him.

He shook his head as he lifted the bottle and carried it back to join the others on the bar. It would be a long time before he'd touch it again.

He looked at the couch, saw the photo. Staring at it, he saw an image of them sitting together. She hadn't wheedled it out of him. She'd been great. She'd done exactly what he would have done if he'd seen her sitting in a mood like that. Exactly what he *had* done when she'd gotten herself in such a state about the media.

He picked up Lodo's picture. So he'd told her? He shook his head again. The only thing to do now was make the best of it.

He knew that it was only a matter of time before some nosy investigative journalist or unofficial biographer unearthed it and splashed it all over the media anyway. He'd buried as much as he could of his early life, but there was always someone willing to swap a story for cash. Hadn't he tried that himself in the hunt for Chris Martinez? He was still trying. It was all he had left.

And as soon as Dante came over, after they'd talked through in detail what he had and hadn't found, he'd be back on it—like the relentless bloodhound he was.

Although, he thought as he lifted the whiskey tumbler and made his way through to the kitchen, the hunt for the Martinez brothers was something he'd be keeping to himself. The contacts he'd had to establish, the risks he'd taken to scratch the underbelly of the world they existed in, to breathe that stench again—there was no way he wanted to share any of *that* with Frankie. He barely wanted Dante to be involved. He didn't want her exposed to it and, crucially, he didn't want to increase the risk by widening the circle of knowledge.

No, he'd shared more than enough with her already.

He put the glass in the gleaming empty dishwasher, turned to the coffee machine and started it up. There was no point in trying to claw back what had gone. All he could do now was keep a lid on the rest. And, yes, he'd asked her to stay on here—but after the events of last night maybe that wasn't such a great idea. Not while Dante was due and the chase was still on. Not when he seemed to be in the habit of opening up and blabbing about stuff that no one should have to carry apart from him.

He shook his head again. What *was* it about her that she had got him to open up like that? He'd never even come close to it before. Totally uncharacteristic behaviour. He had quite knowingly left Lodo's picture out in the bedroom, even after she'd asked him about it. With every other woman that picture had been tucked away. He did not sow the seeds of pity—he did not want to harvest their emotions. If he had any sense at all he'd shut his mouth and shut down this obsession that seemed less and less like unfinished business and more and more like an unsolvable problem.

He was getting used to her being here. He was loving the way their bodies were so utterly in tune with one another. He was loving the easy presence she had, sharing space with him. He was loving the ease that she brought to his life rather than the fuss and nonsense of someone like Carmel. But she had to know that there was never going to be anything more than this. She'd started to ask him last night, just before the call from Dante, and they had to finish that conversation soon.

He checked the time. Dante would have partied hard last night, knowing him, so it would be another couple of hours before he was ready to surface. He could get caught up on work, or he could sweat out this hangover with some serious exercise. An hour of running on the beach and then a session with the punching bag should sort him out. Maybe he should wake Frankie and ask her to come running with him? No, maybe not. He could do with some more thinking time. Because 'losing himself' in her just seemed to be adding to the list of problems, not solving any.

He ran for miles. Kept going well past the point where he normally doubled back. The surfers were out in force, riding the pretty big waves that spilled up and soaked him time and again as he pounded along the beach. A couple of riders passed, their horses galloping in the foam, and he made a mental note to take Frankie out riding in the surf before she left. She'd love it.

His head was still pounding, and still full of conflicting thoughts, but at least he'd cleared up one thing and he felt a hell of a lot better for it.

He trudged up from the beach, thinking about a long drink and a cool shower. Thinking about whether it should be alone or not. Thinking about Frankie and the conversation he was definitely going to have with her. Picking up from where they'd left off last night. God knew he had said it often enough in the past—no commitment past a sexual relationship. No expectations. And definitely no one getting any ideas about buying a hat. He liked her. A lot. But it was best if they were both really clear about what was going to happen next. He had to make sure she had no stupid notions brewing after last night.

But first he was going to get that drink.

He rounded the corner of the garden onto the terrace—right into the middle of a cosy scene.

Dante and Frankie. They were huddled together, staring at something. And the closeness of them, shoulder to shoulder, thigh to thigh on the swing seat, brought a bitter taste to his mouth. What was Dante playing at? Happy families?

'Oh, my God, he's not going to like this.'

'Not going to like what?' he asked, aware of the growl in his voice—aware and not giving a damn.

They both looked up sharply. Dante couldn't hide the moment of surprise on his face, but then, as ever, he slipped right back into easy charm.

'Hey, bro, that's some dynamo you're operating. Wall-to-wall private partying and a ten-mile run before breakfast? I've been here for ages, waiting for you. Good job Frankie was here to look after me.'

Don't let him wind you up, he told himself. But even though he knew Dante was deliberately baiting him, he still rose.

'You're here earlier than I thought,' he said, walking

towards them, still sitting there all cosy together. 'You should have messaged me. I'd have made sure I was here.'

'Well, normally I wouldn't rush, as you know, but with Frankie here just now I can hardly stay away.'

Frankie laughed and punched the side of his arm playfully. 'You're hilarious. You only just got here!'

And then Dante slid his arm around her and squeezed her against his side, blue eyes flashing and smile beaming. A look of complete joy on his face.

'This is still early for me, sweet cheeks. Normally my first meal after Turlington is dinner. Today I'm going for brunch. Impressed?'

Rocco was so, so *un*impressed. Dante had gone right past flirting and moved into some kind of buddy brother-in-law role. The last thing Frankie needed was any more in the way of invitations to be part of Team Hermida. Rocco needed to bring him up to speed on things—and fast.

'Frankie, can you leave us for a moment? Dante and I have a little business to discuss. In private.'

Which was true, but he could have handled it a lot less awkwardly than that, he supposed. The look that flashed over her face told him he'd hurt her, but she rose up with a serene little smile.

'I'll leave you to it. I'd better say goodbye, Dante— I'm not sure when I'll next see you. I have to get back to work soon.'

He stood, too, grabbed her shoulders and held her.

'Ah, parted so soon…I didn't realise. Sorry—I thought you were here for a while. Okay… Well, I'm sure this will only be a temporary goodbye—and it would be great to keep in touch anyway. Hermanos Hermida is always on the lookout for new cheerleaders.'

Had he lost his mind? What the *hell* was he doing?

Rocco watched as Dante pulled her in for a squeeze that lasted far too long, and had the fists in his hands curled into tight, angry balls. If that punching bag was at hand it would get a blasting!

Finally he let her go, and she sauntered off with that sexy little walk, wearing yet another of his shirts. Beautifully.

He turned to Dante.

'*Sweet-cheeks? Cheerleader?* What the hell are you up to, Dante? Since when do you lead *any* woman on to thinking they're going to be part of this family?'

Dante walked towards him.

'Relax. You're like a caged beast. I had to smooth over *your* clumsy move. What was all that about? Sending her away the way you did? Who treats the woman they love like *that*?'

He froze. Dante had sat down again and picked up a newspaper, flicked it open and started to scan through it. He lifted a cup of coffee to his mouth and sipped. As if he had merely asked him about the weather instead of firing a volley of emotionally charged bullets. And striking his target—bull's eye.

'You can forget *that*.'

'What?' he asked, flicking on, sipping on. 'Are you going to try to pretend you're *not* in love with her? It's as obvious as Carmel's fake boobs. Talking of which— you might want to break the habit of a lifetime and check out the latest media reports. If you say you're not in love, you'd better put out a press release.'

And he tossed him his phone.

Pictures of him and Frankie. His eyes scanned them— leaving the villa, entering the Turlington Club, and then the one that he himself had staged, kissing passionately. His eyes widened at how hot they looked. And then there were more—of them staring into each other's eyes, thinking they were unobserved, smiling and hugging. Okay, it *did* look like love caught on camera, but they were just lovers out together. It was no big deal. He'd been with other dates before and there were probably dozens of pictures just like these.

But as his fingers scrolled down he saw what Dante was pointing out. There *were* pictures of him with other women, but he held them at a distance and his face was rigid. And the headlines screamed, The Hurricane Has Been Tamed!

La Gaya—the Magpie—that was what they were calling Frankie, thanks to her striking dark hair and her pearl-pale skin—and to stealing from the nest of the glorious Carmel. *Brilliant*. Just what he needed.

He tossed Dante his phone.

'It'll blow over. No big deal. There's more important stuff to deal with. Like what did you find out?'

Dante dropped the humour like a soaked blanket.

'It was the longest of long shots. Might still be something in it, but I don't know. I got the feeling from our guy that they're doing as much fishing as we are. Someone's claimed to have shared a cell with a guy who knew Chris Martinez. Said he'd been inside and then released after only serving a couple of months. The talk was that he'd done a deal and been given a new identity. But that's all it was. Talk.'

'Sounds pretty likely, though.'

'Maybe. I'm not sure. But there was nothing else to get from the guy. He didn't have any more intel on Martinez. And he started to ask too many other questions. I reckon he was fishing for info about *you*.'

Rocco mulled that over. He'd been so careful about this. He didn't deal directly with investigators himself.

This was the first time Dante had stepped in for him but otherwise he always used a proxy, kept his distance, organised everything via a separate email account and phone number. The last thing he wanted was to bring any shame on the Hermida family. Not after all they'd done for him. So for all that he was picking through the detritus of a nasty world, he'd done it carefully—*very* carefully—up until now.

'Okay,' he said. 'Thanks.'

'What next?'

Rocco rubbed the back of his neck, stretched out his shoulders, flexed his hands. Shook his head.

'I don't know. I'll give it some thought.'

'Don't you think you should leave it for a while? It's not as if the trail is red-hot. Spend some time with Frankie and fix that before she goes. Don't leave loose ends, or you might…'

He frowned at Dante.

'Might what?'

'Lose her.'

They stared at each other across the table, the newspaper spread out between them like a matador's cloak. And Rocco was definitely the bull.

'I'm just saying—I *know* you. When you get information—*any* information—about Martinez you go into these moods, lash out at people. Like I just saw. And someone like Frankie isn't going to hang around to take it.' He put his hands up in a mock surrender. 'Just sayin'…'

'I've got it covered,' he said.

'I'm sure you have.' Dante reached for him, slapped his back, the way they always did. 'I'm going to head off now. Are you travelling back to BA today? Tomorrow?'

'Later today, if you want a lift. Frankie has a meeting

set up with a trader to check out some aloe samples before she flies back to Madrid.'

He nodded. 'I'll leave you two alone. Time must be precious.'

Dante lifted his phone, drained his coffee and pulled out his car keys. One final slap on the back and then he walked away, tripping down the steps as if he was dancing in a damn Hollywood musical. How did he make every moment of his life look like a movie? He pulled him out of his moods every time.

Rocco smiled to himself. God, he loved that man. He headed indoors. Time to shower, shave and then bundle them both back to La Colorada and their full and frank, no-holds-barred discussion.

Frankie finished the last part of her email and reread it for the tenth time. Her finger hovered for two whole seconds above the keyboard—and then she pressed Send.

Gone. Too late to do anything about it now.

She had taken almost two hours to think it through, come to a final decision and then write the damned thing. Two hours in which she had written out a list of pros and cons that had Rocco Hermida's name in both columns.

Staying here was a pro because it gave her more time with him—time to get to know him better, to explore every part of his fabulous estancia, to go riding, to take in the next polo match and to lie in his arms after it and revel in the gorgeous feeling of being Rocco's girl.

But staying here was also a con, because if she did all of those things it meant that she was going to fall deeper and deeper in love. And she wasn't stupid enough to think that was a two-way street—yet. It might be…in time. But after opening up to her last night, lifting the lid on his box of secrets, he'd slammed it shut again, nailed it down and buried it deeper than it had ever been.

He'd prowled through the house on the phone, moving into empty spaces and closing glass doors, literally shutting her out. He'd spent nearly all morning running on the beach, and a good part of the afternoon in the gym. He'd been curt, verging on rude when Dante had been there, and though he'd apologised he'd offered no explanation or softening. It was almost as if he was angry at himself for sharing his story, for making himself seem a little more human, a little more mortal than godlike.

And in a way that just added to the allure. He was *so* complex, so dark, so vulnerable. And she ached to help him slough off this crown of thorns he wore. She'd never felt more moved than when she was lying in his arms, making love in the early hours of the morning. It was like opening her eyes after the longest sleep, glimpsing a beautiful sunrise, seeing a glorious future—and then feeling darkness seep back as night fell prematurely, suddenly. Leaving her stumbling about in the dark, unable to find the light.

So what to do? What to do…?

In the end one thing had tipped the balance—he enriched her. But more than that he needed her. She knew how hard it had been for him to talk about his early childhood. Maybe he never had before. And if she didn't make an effort for him now she might never take the chance again. Because it *was* a chance. There was no guarantee that he was going to revisit any of that trauma with her or anyone else. It broke her heart to think that he carried that guilt. But it was so *him*. To shoulder everything himself. And keeping everyone else at a distance was probably the only way he could handle it.

Did she really expect him to treat her any differently

than any of the countless women she'd seen on those pictures that she and Dante had scrolled through earlier? She knew what she felt, but getting him to a point where he might admit the same was like trying to reroute a hurricane. It was only going to go where it wanted. And when it hit land everybody had better stand back.

She sighed and clicked on her sent box to confirm that the email had indeed been delivered. Knowing that in approximately two hours' time her boss was going to read it and probably go into some kind of tailspin himself.

The timing couldn't be worse. She was asking for leave at a time when she should have been parcelling herself up to be sent express delivery back to Madrid. She could feel in her bones the resistance to her proposals already. The emails that had been coming from head office were getting more and more cautionary. She could detect a derisory sniff in the air, and now she was seven days away from a one-to-one with her boss.

But she was going to use this extra time to polish her proposal until it shone. Going organic was the only way. Natural products were everywhere. There was nothing to commend Evaña to the modern savvy shopper. If she could develop an organic line and hook in a couple of bloggers, they'd be off to a flyer. If not they were going to continue to lose customers like skin lost elasticity, and none of the big stockists would look twice at them. At least this way the ageing geriatric company might have a future. And if it had a future, so did she.

That *had* to remain her number one priority. Being here with Rocco was enriching, but it wasn't real life. Real life was waiting for her when she jumped out of the metro in Madrid and picked her way along the *calle* to head office and her moment in the spotlight.

She packed up her briefcase in readiness for their

early-morning helicopter ride. Rocco's helicopter... Rocco's pilot. Hopefully their journey would go by unnoticed. The last thing she wanted was any more media interest as a result of her being with him. Her poor mother was already contending with whatever it was that had tipped Danny over the edge and into wedded bliss. He was playing his cards very close to his chest, as he always did. But thankfully what had happened in Punta seemed to be staying in Punta—for now anyway.

She braced herself every time she got a message, thinking it might be her mother, wailing and crossing herself over her daughter's loose morals—or even more likely her father, who would be happy to finally be proved right.

She zipped up the black leather case, stacked it beside the gorgeous old desk in the study she'd settled herself in and smiled. Strange how she'd begun to see things slightly differently after hearing Rocco's words. For a moment she let herself bask in all the sweet things he'd whispered to her at night. Let herself feel that she was unique in a positive way, rather than freakily different from all the local girls. Feel proud of what she'd achieved rather than ashamed that she didn't want what had been mapped out for her. An inspiration, he'd called her once. And more than a tiny part of her wanted to believe that.

She traced her way back through the expansive masculine home. Polished parquet floors with silk runners spread out along long narrow hallways. Console tables punctuated the burgundy silk walls, highlighting fabulous black-and-white photographs of gauchos and dancers and patent-coated stallions. It was so *him*—so darkly, elegantly, brutally beautiful.

His bedroom threw the house's dark arteries into airy relief. High ceilings, wide windows and sumptuous silk carpets—and the bed that they had christened after that disastrous pony ride two days earlier.

She smiled, looked at it and straightened the pony-skin cushions, setting them against the vast wooden headboard. The little photo of Lodo was back in place on the bedside table. She picked it up and looked at it—really looked at it. What a beautiful boy he had been…but so solemn. God only knew what terrors he'd seen—what terrors Rocco had seen and continued to see. He might have clammed up again, but those flashes of truth had given her such insight—personal nuggets she'd hold dear and treasure.

She sighed. Blew out a huge breath she hadn't even realised she'd been holding. She glanced over at the door to the dressing room and her battered little carry-on and suit bags. She had to remember she was here for a purpose, and it wasn't all about taming the Hurricane—and the more she read the subtext of her directors' bulletins the more she felt the enormity of that task, too.

But she *could* nail this, she thought as she moved over and ran a hand down her best summer suit, smoothing down the fabric and straightening the seams. She could actually make a difference—not only to Evaña but to herself, too. She could talk terms with traders, strike reasonable deals and put the stats into a really slick presentation. She could do some groundwork with bloggers and a beauty editor she'd begun to get friendly with. She really could pull this off.

And then she'd have banked more than enough to ride back to County Meath with her head high and her pride intact and demand a very long overdue apology from her father.

CHAPTER ELEVEN

TWENTY-FOUR HOURS LATER Frankie jumped out of the helicopter, kept her head bent, clutched her briefcase to her body and hurled herself across the parched grass to the driveway. Her heels stuck in mud-baked crevices and the rotors thundered over her head, throwing up the skirt of her dress. But she didn't care. She just wanted out of it. Out of the helicopter and away from her stinging reflections on the crucifying day she'd forced herself to relive on the hour-long flight back.

Coming in to land, she'd spotted riders cutting through the head-high grass fields and moving into the rougher countryside that she'd crossed herself a few days earlier. Clouds of dust swirled and settled as they rode through green-and-yellow grassland. Rocco was sure to be with them. She'd left him this morning, after another night of frenzied passion—another night when she'd longed to cry out her heart into the hot dark night, to whisper her love and bask in the emotions that rolled through her when she lay in his arms.

But she hadn't. She'd held back. She'd silently floated in oceans of happiness, but had been ever aware of the crashing waterfall that was right there, just out of sight, a glaring reminder to hold something back—her life raft.

She couldn't criticise Rocco for anything. He was attentive, considerate and caring. He worshipped her body, and he appeared to enjoy her mind, her conversation and her company. But he was as deep and as distant as ever. Every time she'd tried to sneak a look past his barricades he'd somehow made them higher.

And now, with the days ticking by, she was feeling more and more anxious that she'd made a terminal career mistake by asking for more time when the finance department was asking for more cutbacks.

But she'd left this morning determined to bring back some good news, to make the directors see that she really knew what she was doing.

Before that she and Rocco had breakfasted on the north-facing terrace, surrounded by huge potted urns of showy red flowers and under the arches of clambering ivy that softened the house and the wide, spare landscape. Silently, comfortably, they'd munched on freshly made bread, sipping strong coffee and planning their day, so full of promise and excitement.

Rocco had planned a morning of intense demanding phone calls to finally nail the squirming management of Mendoza Vineyard, and then an afternoon of wild riding across his land. He'd promised to wait until she returned so she could join him. That had been the plan. And she had been desperate to saddle up the other mare—Roisin—and see just how much like her mother she was. In fact she had jumped right into his lap with joy at the thought of it, and he had gifted her one of his rare laughs, his face lighting with happiness, his eyes sparkling with pleasure.

Frankie had never felt more alive. Today was going to be *her* day. She was going in well armed after her visit to the traders in the Dominican Republic. She knew what she wanted, the terms she could afford to offer. The processing plants were nearer at hand, and the botanicals they needed were all available locally, too. The opportunity to make genuinely organic products rather than to follow the market leaders with their petrochemical derivatives was just too good to miss. She could visualise the artwork, smell the creams and lotions, feel the luxury...

So where had it all gone wrong?

Along the wide, straight jacaranda-lined driveway she stumble marched. Sweat and dust and her own gritty determination were smeared all across her face. Her mascara had run about three hours earlier. She'd seen it when she had tried to stare herself calm in the bathrooms of the one-storey cubic office block. When she'd excused herself after an excruciating meeting between the trader who'd gathered all the samples she'd asked for and an audience she hadn't.

Staring into that mirror, her best suit a crumpled mess, her hair blown all over, she had felt again the crippling sense that she was once more a silly little girl playing in a big boys' world.

La Gaya—one of them had openly called her that. Magazines with Carmel de Souza's picture had been clearly laid out on the reception area's coffee table. One of the traders, his arms folded over his chest, had set his face in amused judgement. So *this* was the Hurricane's lover? Not much to see. Not compared to Carmel.

Either they hadn't known she was fluent in Spanish or they hadn't cared. The terms they'd offered had been unmanageable. The profit margins and her hopes of promotion had slid away like oil through her fingers as she'd contemplated their bottom line. It had been hopeless.

All this time, all this work, and the whole thing was now unravelling out of her control. And she suspected that more than some of the reason for the unreasonable terms was her relationship with Rocco. Who would take her seriously when she was, after all, just another morsel of arm candy?

She'd kept it together for as long as she could—she really had. She knew there was no place for emotion in business. Especially when she was there representing her company. So she'd taken it on the chin until she'd heard 'La Gaya' one last time. Then she'd stood up, snapped her tablet closed, braced her hands on the desk and fired at them with both barrels.

She hadn't come all the way across the Atlantic Ocean to listen to this rubbish. They were in business or they weren't. And the last thing—the *very* last thing—that a prestigious, established firm like Evaña would do was get into bed with a bunch of half-baked professionals like them!

She reached the lakes that marked the start of the house grounds proper. Willows overhung the water, fronds dripping down, gently scoring the water's surface. Huge puffy clouds bounced their way across the sky. So much nature and not a living soul to be seen. Good. That was just what she needed right now.

She pulled her phone out of her bag as she marched, checking to see if there were any messages. Not trusting herself to call Rocco, she had sent him a text.

I'll pass on the riding. See you later.

No kiss. She'd ignored his call and climbed back into the helicopter, feeling twenty-year-old pain all over again. Fury at not being taken seriously; rage that she wasn't considered equal. Like when she'd been her brothers' shadow, following them about the farm, until her father had caught her and sent her off to the kitchen, roaring at her that she was getting in the way—a liability, a pest.

She flung open the front doors and clicked her way along the parquet. Heels deadened in the rugs, she passed the photos of sullen gauchos, passed the console table now groaning under the weight of Rocco's boxing trophies. She'd found them the day before, in a box in the dressing room, and polished them up happily and set them out proudly as he'd watched, humouring her.

She pushed her way into the bedroom and stood there. And breathed. And stared around.

Rocco's bedroom. Rocco's house.

What was she *doing*? What on *earth* was she doing?

Still behaving as if she was six years old—running away from her problems. Hiding out in her bedroom until she stopped crying and then flying back outdoors on a pony or after her brothers, only this time being much more careful not to get caught.

But she wasn't in her own bedroom. She wasn't even in her own country. She was here because she'd contrived to be.

Like dawn breaking over frosty fields, suddenly everything sparkled with clarity. She walked to the bed and sank down.

She really had brought this on herself. The whole nine yards of it. The trip to South America. She'd been doggedly, determinedly desperate to come here. *Desperada*. He was right. She had done all this for *him*. Right from dreaming up the new range, so dependent on natural products... She could have gone to India or Africa. But no, she'd found the best plantations in Argentina. And no one had been able to persuade her otherwise.

She'd planned and plotted the whole thing. Including the polo match. How could she have been so blind that she hadn't seen for herself what she was doing? So she was *over* Rocco Hermida? *Hated* the man who had broken her heart and stolen her pony? Who was she fooling? She had *never* gotten over him. And every move she'd made in the past four days had guaranteed she never would.

Blind…? Stupid…?

Now she had to add those to the mix.

She was ambitious, yes—but even she hadn't realised how much. And now the whole thing was coming tumbling round her head. She'd veered off her career path and right into the path of the Hurricane. Even though she'd known it would be short-term, even though she'd been able to see the devastation that was bound to be wreaked.

She was all kinds of a fool. If she didn't act fast she was going to blow her future with Evaña. It was time she grew up. It was time she stopped waiting for Rocco. She'd chased her dream all the way here. And her dream was as out of reach as it had ever been.

Because what was *Rocco* doing? Was *he* pining in his bedroom, head under the pillow, wailing like a baby? No. Damn right he wasn't. He was out on the pampas, wind in his hair, riding up a storm. He was no closer to her emotionally than he had been that very first night.

She had seen into the depths of his despair, had tried to soothe and salve. She could see how much hurt he harboured and she could help him through it—she knew she could. But he would not let her in.

Lodo's picture was there. Rocco's mind was not. Every time she tried he backed right off.

She had gone out on a limb professionally and now, instead of ticking off her to-do list, she was actually unravelling all her efforts. She wasn't just putting things on hold, she was deconstructing them. Getting her face splashed all across the media and then erupting when an ill-mannered man made some stupid comments. Had she learned *nothing*? Had she left the farm, travelled round the world, fought her way to a position of relative success just to have it all shatter around her?

An inspiration?

A devastation, more like. She *had* to get her act together and salvage what was left. Get back on the career path. Limit the damage. Batten down the hatches and hold tight.

What a day! How long since he'd allowed himself the luxury of taking off for the afternoon? Riding out around his land, feeling free, feeling part of a bigger scene, a higher purpose? Feeling that the world was his and that peace was…possible. He'd wanted Frankie there—he'd waited for her—but there would be other times. Perhaps.

As he'd ridden out through dust clouds and stony streams he'd had time to think, to curse himself for not being as straight with her as he should have been. The emails she'd gotten from her boss had crushed her. Panicked her. Adding to that by laying it out that what they had was at best a one-week sexual odyssey had seemed too cruel. And the more time he spent with her, the more he began to wonder if this *might* actually work longer term… It might—but he had to be absolutely honest with himself and with her.

He wasn't the marrying type. He wasn't even the commitment type. And she was. She might not admit it, even to herself, but she was the type of girl who put down roots, built a nest, cultivated life in a way that he recognised. If things had been different he might have wanted it, too. Real depth…real values. A real person. She wasn't going to flit about like an overpainted butterfly, landing on flowers, looking for attention like all the other women he'd dated.

He paused at that. Had he dated them for that very reason? So there would be no genuine commitment? Possibly. But Frankie was different. So was he being fair to her? Because it wasn't going to end any other way. He'd made that promise to himself years back. Being responsible for other human beings was not something he did well. Hell, the only reason he and Dante were so close now was because of the utter devastation he had caused every time he'd run away.

Two years his junior, Dante had hung on his every word, so when his efforts to get back to the streets had become wilder and wilder, when he'd seen just how upset he'd made Dante every time he was dragged back to his life of luxury—all that emotional blackmail had been banked and paid out again in brotherly bonding. They'd used Dante as a weapon to tame him. But that manipulation, that responsibility for someone else was never going to happen again.

So had he given Frankie false hope with his drunken blurting about Lodo? Sharing his emotional detritus for her to pick over? Who knew? He'd expected her to be flying high on some emotional magic carpet the next day, looking for him to jump on and relive it all over again. He'd been on his guard for pitying looks, stage-managed conversations, trailing pauses. No way was he going to indulge in any review of *that* particular episode.

It was time to face up to having the inevitable conversation that had eluded them so far. To go on any longer without talking through the state of play was disingenuous. The last thing he wanted was for her to build their time together into more than a week of fantastic sex—to set any emotional store by the fact that they'd each had their confessional moments…in his case a once-in-a-lifetime confessional moment.

But he'd be fooling himself if he didn't admit how much he hoped she'd share his point of view and keep things ticking along as they were. If she was cool with a physical relationship—a monogamous physical relationship—he was right there with her.

He walked from the yard to the house, already thinking about where she would be. What they'd do as soon as they met. He'd decanted the 2006 and 2003 Malbecs from Mendoza—could almost taste the subtle soft fruits and the plump warm spices. A couple of steaks, the fabulous wine and then an evening together in exactly the same way they'd shared every previous one. Perfect.

The house was empty. Usually the gauchos and grooms inhabited the kitchen and the rooms on the south wing, but since Frankie had taken up residence they had made themselves scarce. Another unnecessary line in the sand, he thought, kicking off his boots, pulling his shirt over his head and twisting the lid from a bottle of water. People were reading more into this than they should.

He walked on through the house. Alone.

She'd have been back for a good two hours now. Hot tub? Terrace? Bed?

He drew a sharp breath through his teeth and felt himself tighten as every sweet little image formed in his mind. This separation, if only for a few hours, had done them good. He was half crazy with longing for her. Strange that she hadn't wanted to come out riding. He reckoned things at work had maybe piled up for her. He *had* monopolised her time, and after all she was here on business. Even if that business *was* a bit sparse.

He'd done a bit of digging. Just a bit. And he wouldn't be holding his breath that her efforts were going to pay off. Or *any* efforts. Evaña was a company heading in the wrong direction, and Frankie dragging herself along in the dirt as it stuttered to the end wasn't going to be her smartest career move.

But that was *her* business. There would be nothing to be gained by him voicing that opinion.

The bedroom was empty. He seized the chance and had a quick shower, soaping himself alone for the first time in days. Strange how he'd got so acclimatised to her being around… Strange that he didn't resent it.

In fact as he tossed the damp towel into the laundry bin and pulled on fresh clothes an irritation that he'd never felt before barked up, unbidden. Where the hell *was* she? She should have been there to meet him.

His calls through the house echoed back unanswered. He checked his phone, checked his messages, but there were none from her.

Five minutes later he found her. Coiled on the ancient leather sofa in his favourite room—the snug. It was the room that had been his bedroom when he'd first bought the estancia. His bedroom, living room and kitchen. He'd existed in there as he had slowly ripped out and rebuilt the place, brick by brick. He'd made this room habitable first, then a bathroom. Then the stables.

For a long time the stables had been way more luxurious than the house. His horses deserved that. They were his everything. He poured his love—what there was of it—into them. He owed them everything. Without them he was nothing. He owed them for every envious glance from a polo player, every roar of adulation from the crowd. For each and every sponsorship deal that had opened doors and fast-tracked him to his other business deals.

People didn't understand that. Leaving behind the

luxury of the Hermida estancia had been like fleeing a gilded cage. He'd been thought mad to walk away. But his parents had understood. And Dante. They had understood everything, supported him in everything. He'd left that 'safe house' with one pony—Siren, his eighteenth birthday present. And after that he'd headed to Europe. Met Frankie in Ireland. Life had taken off. He would never, ever repay that debt. But he would never stop trying.

Frankie. She had to have heard him coming in but she kept her head buried in her laptop, brows knitted and a strange swirl of tension all around her.

She still didn't look up.

'Hey...I missed you out riding.'

He walked over to her, the dusky evening already softening every surface, blurring the odds and ends of dark artisan furniture against the plaster walls.

He leaned over her, kissed the top of her head, lifted her chin with his finger and met her lips. He could taste slight resistance, but it was nothing that he couldn't melt in moments.

And he did.

She sighed against his mouth.

'I missed you out riding, too.'

He kissed her, revelling in the 'Hi, honey, I'm home' greeting between them. He could get quite used to this.

'I waited. But there will be other times.'

She pulled herself back, dipped her head, stared at the screen.

So she was in a mood—prickly, like a neglected pony, one who'd expected to be ridden at a match but had been swapped for another. Sulky and jagged. Playing hard to get. Okay. He could deal with that.

He lifted her laptop onto the couch and scooped his

hands under her arms, lifted her up. Her reluctant hands slid around his neck.

'So what happened? How was your day? Did it go as well as you hoped?'

Her eyes rolled and her mouth tightened into a grim little slash.

'Not quite. Walking into an AGM of the Carmel Fan Club wasn't quite what I had in mind.'

He frowned. 'What does *that* mean?'

This time she pulled herself totally out of his arms, slid back down onto the couch, lifted up her laptop again—as if it was some kind of guard dog and he should back right off.

'Just what I said. There was quite a welcoming committee—seemed as though the traders had got the whole company out in force to see how I measured up. I had to wait in the reception area—and guess what were all over the coffee table? Celebrity magazines dedicated to your airhead ex. It was heartfelt—it really was.'

'I'm sure it was coincidental,' he said, thinking how unlike her this spiteful tone was.

'*Are* you? Were you *there*?'

He looked at her. Weighed up the benefit of engaging in this. Decided against it.

He turned round, shook his head and went off to the dining room. The wine decanters were set as he'd left them. Each vintage the perfect temperature, opened to breathe for the optimum length of time. He lifted the 2006. It was mooted to be even plummier than the 2003, and he held it to what remained of the light. These were *his* wines now. And there would be better and better to come.

How long had he harboured a desire to be *that* Argen-

tinian? The one whose heritage went so far back. The
one who had fought and risen above hardship. One who
didn't have to worry about a place to sleep, a mouth to
feed. A reputation to uphold. How remarkable that with
effort you could *buy* that kind of stability. And he had.
Centuries of tradition, and he now held it in his hand.
How proud would his *mamá* and *papá* be now? How
proud Lodo?

He swallowed his self-indulgent reflections, selected
two etched antique-crystal glasses and made his way
back to Frankie. She would enjoy these. She would ap-
preciate the effort and pride that had gone into them.

The room was darkening with each passing moment.
He reached for the control pad and flicked a switch.
Lamps in corners began to glow softly. He turned. The
sheen on Frankie's dipped head gleamed. She looked
right. There on that couch, in this room. Slowly, rever-
ently, he poured, the full, fabulous scents wafting up as
the liquid sloshed. He paced to her, handed her a glass.

'Try this.'

She made a face as though it was an old tin cup of
stagnant water. Reluctantly held out her hand. Why did
she not know what this represented for him? She was
normally so attuned to him...

He watched as she swirled the dark red liquid round
the bulbous bottomed glass as if it was a science lesson.

He did the same, but sank his nose in for a proper
smell.

'What do you think of this vintage? This is the 2006
Malbec. The season went on until April that year. The
aromas are immense—so balanced, no?'

Frankie stilled her eyes, cast her mouth into a tight
little moue. 'Yes, it's amazing.'

Suddenly he felt a spark of anger.

'No, what's *amazing* is your churlish attitude.'

She did a double-take.

'What? What did you say?'

He sighed. How to phrase this without turning it into the drama she was clearly spoiling for?

'Frankie, the existence of Carmel de Souza in this world has nothing to do with you. I saw how you let her presence affect you at the party, but surely you're smarter than to let a photograph of her affect you at your *work*?'

Her back was against the huge armrest of the couch. Her legs were curled up, knees bent. He watched her from the corner of his eye as he stared straight ahead, twirling the gorgeous liquor round and round, examining the patina on the glass as it sank back down before being swirled up again.

'It's only *because* of that damn party that I'm feeling like this,' she said, cold steel jarring every word. 'If I hadn't been paraded about in front of all those cameras nobody would've even known who I was.'

She thrust her legs out, bare. She was wearing a T-shirt and shorts—not one of his shirts, he noticed. She gripped her laptop, held it steady on her lap.

'I went down there today as a professional and came back as nothing other than the Hurricane's current sex pet. And not a very impressive one at that.'

He raised his eyebrow—the only sign that he'd registered her statement. She needed to calm the hell down.

He swirled the wine one more time before drawing long on the scent and then finally tasting.

'I bought this vineyard today. I've always been a fan of their wines.'

She fumed. Obviously.

'Great.'

'Meaning…?'

'Meaning that it's all in a day's work for you to go shopping for a vineyard. Did anyone pile in to look at you and judge you? Make you feel as if you'd won last place in the celebrity-girlfriend competition? And that you were an idiot for getting your photo all over the front pages of some trashy magazine?'

'No, because the only person who judges me is *me*. I choose who I sleep with, and it's of no interest to me what anyone thinks of that.'

She reared up. The laptop slid to the couch. Her wine sloshed up the sides of the glass. She glanced at it and reached to put it on the side table, missed its edge in the gloom of the room. The glass wobbled and he lunged for it, caught it in his hand and righted it.

She opened her mouth, clamped it shut, then opened it again.

'That's all I am to you. Isn't it?'

Halfway to his mouth, he stalled the progress of his own glass. So there it was. The gauntlet thrown down. All hope of a mature, considered conversation was gone— Frankie's self-deprecating emotional show had just rolled into town.

'*Isn't* it?' She stepped down from the couch, the shrill tone in her voice a sword being drawn from its sheath.

He lowered the glass.

'We are currently lovers, if that's what you mean.'

She stood within the circle of his personal space. If he reached for her she would fit his body perfectly. He would curl her into him and lay his chin on her head. She would press her head to his chest and then plant tiny kisses on his neck. She would clamber up him like a cat and he would hold her, carry her, make love to her and know that he had never before and never would again find a girl like her.

But standing here right now, less than eighteen inches apart, it was like being on either side of a crevice. One wrong move and the whole thing would disappear down into a chasm. Gone.

'We are "currently lovers"?' she repeated, the low tone of her voice unmistakable.

He would not give her more. *Would not.*

He looked at her, at the damp, dusky lashes closed over the huge hazel eyes that had gazed into his, at the small soft lips that had given him every type of pleasure imaginable, at the silken swish of hair that had lain across his body night after night. At the selfless, giving, generous, loving girl that she was...

She loved him. He knew it then. As she stood there right in front of him. An iron hand squeezed his heart and a steel glaze crept all over his skin. She loved him and he could not love her back.

Not in the way she deserved.

'We can stay as lovers...like this...' His voice was strained, as though the decade-old tannins in the wine had welded it shut. The glass now dangled at the end of his arm, preventing him from holding her. He *should* hold her. He should comfort her. Every second that ticked by deepened the chasm. But still he held the glass in his hand, cupped the delicate weighted ball of crystal.

'Like what?'

One foot hovered over the edge.

He straightened his shoulders. Drew in a breath.

'Frankie...' he began, and he saw by the glimmer of hope that had flashed in her eyes and then slid down her face that she already knew what was coming next. If only he could save her, not pull her with him into the chasm...

'Frankie, we're great together…'

She closed her eyes. Clamped them shut as if trying to block him out.

'But…?' she breathed. 'We're great together *but*…?' Every syllable rang with the dreadful, sonorous clang of defeat. 'What are you telling me? What glib, half-baked reason are you going to trot out?'

'Angel, please,' he said, feeling the earth now leaving him, knowing that they were both falling.

She opened her eyes, looked at his arm, his shoulder, at a spot on the wall. In the distance he could hear the rumble of threatened thunder. A summer storm passing overhead. The land would be refreshed by morning, the air clearer and lighter. But he could already feel the aching black pain that would live in his heart as he rode the land, knowing she wouldn't be there for him to come back to.

'Shall I make it easy for you?'

She didn't sound angry anymore—just desperately, desperately sad.

'We're great together because we have great sex. But that's all there is and all there ever will be. We don't work on any other level.'

'That's not true,' he bit out.

She looked at him then. His Frankie. A dark sweep of hair hung over one eye, her stubborn chin was raised, her hazel eyes sunken and saddened.

'It is, Rocco. You're carrying around so much baggage, but everyone pretends it's not there. Even Dante— even *he* skips over all your moods and sulks. And God knows who you'd ever let get closer than him. A woman? A "weak little woman"?'

'We *are* close, Frankie.'

'I don't feel it, Rocco. Not close enough.'

In the past five minutes the gap between them had widened and stretched. They were still standing in each other's space, but light years apart—like dying stars in the cosmic darkness.

He swallowed. Words to beg her to stay—on *his* terms—words to beg her forgiveness for not being able to give her what she needed, words to erase the mask of pain he saw settle into the beautiful curves of her face, already gaunt and sunken—those words stuck deep in his throat. And his mouth sealed over them, bottled them up like uncorked wine.

She turned away as a huge sob forced her shoulders to shudder.

He'd save her. If he *could* save her. Give her the water and light that she needed. But she would always be parched of his love. His arms hung limp at his sides as she finally stepped from their space, bent for her laptop and left.

He stood in his room, the heart of his home, while the one chance he'd ever had of feeling true love slipped like a ghost from his grasp.

It always came back to this. It didn't matter about walls or wealth. None of that mattered. He'd never felt happier than in the warmth of his *mamá*'s bed until he'd felt the warmth of Frankie. A cardboard bed cuddled up with Lodo…sleeping on the beach with Frankie. It was people that mattered. But she mattered too much for him to give her only half a life.

The glass in his hand weighed cannonball-heavy. He lifted it now, looked at the delicate white patterns cut out of the paper-thin crystal. He looked at the barely touched, carefully nursed vintage wine that coated and glazed the sides of the glass. Looked at the space on the couch. Moments ago he'd cared more about scents and flavours than the beautiful woman who'd sat there.

And then, with all his might, he lifted it past his head and heaved it at the wall.

And watched as the rich red liquid streaked down the plaster.

CHAPTER TWELVE

SUNDAY MORNINGS AT home hadn't changed much in all these years. Frankie lay in her narrow single bed, staring at the low sloping ceiling as the scents of lunch wafted upstairs. Chicken and potatoes would be roasting; pan lids would be wobbling with vegetables boiling underneath. The windows would be steamed up and her mother's rosy face would be peering into the oven, or she'd be wiping her damp hands on the cloth tucked into her apron.

In the lounge, only ever used on high days and holidays, her father would be marooned in a sea of Sunday papers like a grumpy old walrus, occasionally barking out his horror at what he read to anyone who cared to listen. Such was their life—the cosy, comfortable, mundane life that they'd shared for almost forty years.

Why had she felt horror at the prospect of such a life? Why had she fought against it every step of the way? Casting her net as far from this place as she possibly could. Determined never to be *that* woman, *that* wife.

Why—when she knew, now that it was so far from her grasp, that it was as important to her as all her other dreams. Maybe even more so...

Perhaps not here on a farm in County Meath, but maybe on an estancia in Argentina. Or in a studio apartment in Madrid. Anywhere, in fact, as long as it was with Rocco.

She rolled around in the narrow bed, tucking her legs in sharply when shafts of cold air scored them. Her head was under her pillow, a balled-up paper handkerchief clutched in her fist. When would the crying stop? When would the misery of knowing she would never be with him again finally ease?

She felt the thickening in her nose and the heat behind her eyes that warned her of another outpouring. Two weeks she'd been like this. One week in Spain, and then she'd finally caved and taken leave, coming back here for the holidays.

That week in Spain had been a blur, of course. She'd caught the Madrid flight she'd originally booked, much to the discomfort of her fellow passengers and the aircrew, who hadn't quite known what to do with the agonised bundle of limbs she'd become, sleeping and weeping her way across the Atlantic.

Then, appearing for work, it had turned out she hadn't needed the extra time after all—though God knew they'd encouraged her to take it when they'd seen that their waterproof mascara wasn't quite so waterproof after all.

It was a miracle that she'd pulled herself together and finally got her moment in front of the board. Skirting over her lack of information about the Argentina growers, she'd made a one-sided, half-hearted presentation about the potentials of the Dominican Republic and openly accepted, when questioned that, yes, she *had* become 'overwrought' during her meeting with the Argentinian traders. And worse, yes—they probably could get better terms from India.

But Rocco Hermida wasn't in India.

He wasn't anywhere now.

And it was time she finally realised that. Since he'd walked out of her life she'd been chasing him. They were *his* steps she'd followed. *He* was the reason she'd cast her net so far and wide. *He* was the reason she'd taken a gap year, gone travelling, set herself higher and higher goals. She'd emulated him. She'd wanted to be worthy of him, even if she couldn't actually have him.

The only incredible part was how blind she had been in not seeing all this before. And, even more worryingly, persisting for all those years when she should have realised as he'd slung his rucksack over his shoulder that morning ten years ago that he didn't need her. Never would.

Tears burned and flowed again. The black jaws of agony yawned awake inside her again. She pushed her fist into her mouth to stop the howl. Her teeth scored her flesh, but the numb sting of pain meant nothing. She curled into a little ball and rocked herself into another day without him.

Eventually she became aware of someone moving about in the hallway. Her father, clearing his throat— his passive-aggressive way of telling her that she should be downstairs helping her mother.

Well, he was right about that. But that was *all* he was right about.

Since she'd come back they'd quietly circled one another, silently assessing but not engaging. She knew it upset her mother, but she was putting so much effort into not crying in front of them that she couldn't risk getting involved in any arguments with him. But it was coming. She could feel it.

Slowly she sat up, dropped her legs out of the bed, let them dangle in the chilly air. How many times had she sat just like this over the years? Countless. And here she was again. She stood. Her heart was strong. It could beat seventy times a minute. It had just taken the pummelling of her life and it was still beating. Life was going to get better. It *had* to.

She shuffled her feet into slippers, shrugged her shoulders into Mark's old Trinity College hoody and began to make her way along the hall.

'So you're going to join us?'

He was standing at the top of the stairs—just like he'd been all those years ago. Just standing there. Staring. Judging.

'Yes,' she said.

Something about his dark, solid, unflinching outline made her pause her steps. He was holding something in his hand.

'I *knew* I was right. All these years…'

There was barely any light in the top hallway. A tiny skylight and a four-paned window at the end. The flower-printed shade that her brothers had to dodge as they passed held only a dim lightbulb that daubed the walls and carpet in dark beige patches the colour of cold tea. Her father's anger radiated its own dark gloom.

She stared at him. The default denial—*No, Daddy, I promise I didn't*—sank to the floor. She had no use for it anymore.

'Yes. You were right. Does that make you happy?'

He seemed to take that like a blow, tipping his head back slightly with the shock of it. She couldn't see his face properly, but she could sense the intake of breath.

'Happy? How could any shame you bring on yourself make me *happy*? Then or now?'

'I've never done *anything* shameful.' She jerked her chin up at him. And she hadn't. There was no shame in love. 'But God knows you made me feel like I did. Treating me like an outcast—sending me away like that.'

'It was for your own good.'

'How can you *say* that? You ruined my life—selling my pony and imprisoning me in that convent.'

'Your life wasn't ruined by that—you were doing a good-enough job of that on your own. And you know we had to sell her. No one regretted it as much as I. But there was no option. Not with the run of bad luck we'd had with the others. And then Danny leaving. And anyway, the convent was the making of you.'

The convent was the making of you? He really thought that? The convent hadn't been the making of her—it had been her life outdoors, the farm, nature all around. It had been leaving home and travelling, choosing a job in a country where she barely spoke the language. Highest paths, toughest challenges, always proving herself. Hadn't it?

'You were wild. Ran wild from before you could walk. You needed some anchors and there were none strong enough. The nuns trained you to stand still and focus yourself.'

She almost had to steady herself as her world was suddenly whipped up in the air and reordered.

'I thought that you'd calmed down completely when you landed that job. But clearly not. The minute *he* appears you're all over the place again.'

He thrust forward a magazine, held it in his hand like a folded weapon. She stared at it. He thrust it farther.

'Read it. See what they're printing. And *then* tell me you're not ashamed.'

She lifted the magazine—the gossip section from his Sunday paper. She could barely make out the text, but his finger jabbed at a photograph and she could see by the stark colours exactly what it was.

The Turlington Club party. She was in white. Rocco was in black. She lifted it closer, tilted it to catch the gloomy brown light, and felt the fist around her heart squeeze a little tighter. Rocco was holding her as if they were dancing the most erotic tango. Bodies like licks of fire. Heat and light and passion bounced from the page. She turned away, clutching it, staring at it.

'It's him, isn't it? The one who came here. The hotshot…'

She stared at the picture. Stared at the man who was her whole world.

Her father was droning on and on. 'Coming here… turning your head like that…leading you on…getting you to do…'

She was suddenly jolted out of her gloom.

'Rocco didn't lead me on. What are you *saying*? It was me who tried to lead *him* on.'

The words her father was about to growl out hung in his mouth unsaid and he gaped.

She looked at him. 'Have you thought for all these years that *he* was the one to blame for what happened that night?'

Across the gloom of the afternoon they stared at each other. She was barely aware of the television being turned off, a door closing softly downstairs.

'It was me who went to him. *I* went to him. And then I went back to him last month.'

She saw him swallow—heard it, too. A gulp of shock.

For a moment he looked puzzled, even hurt. Then his face gathered itself into the storm that never seemed far away.

'Well, why have you come back here now?'

His voice was low and cold, like sleet landing on mud. But as she heard it and felt it all the darkness slowly began to melt away. She looked down at the magazine in her hand. She'd had all that. All that man. *Her* man. The only one who was right for her. All she'd lacked was the patience to help him see that, too.

'You know, Dad, I've no idea why I came back here. Not for your support or your love anyway.'

'Pfff!' he said. 'If we didn't love you we wouldn't care that you get yourself into all this trouble. You *and* your brother.'

For a moment he looked at her and she saw the shadows of worry and care etched deep. He was so hidebound by what others saw that he couldn't see that love was the most valuable commodity of all. He should be *happy* that Danny had got married in Dubai. So what if it wasn't a traditional wedding? It wasn't 'trouble'—it was love.

She thought of Rocco's hands holding her, his lips loving her. She thought of their nights and days. She thought of him gently teasing her out of her silly insecurities and stubbornly hiding his. She thought of him with Dante, his flashes of jealousy. His tiny keepsake photograph of Lodo. His overwhelming loyalty. And his love. He had such a capacity for love. He was frightened of it, but it was there in everything he did for them. And for her. He couldn't hide it. He loved her. He needed her.

'He loves me,' she whispered to herself. 'He understands me. He would never do anything to hurt me.'

'Well, if he loves you so much why are you here? Why aren't you with him? Why hasn't he made an honest woman of you instead of all this parading about, getting your picture in the papers, giving those gossips in the village something to say about you?'

She looked away from her father—out at the December sky.

'He made an honest woman of me the first day I met him. He showed me who I am and he made me learn about myself in a way that no one else possibly could.'

And he had. Her sexuality was part of her—a part of which she was now proud. They were perfectly matched, true partners, but each of them carried such huge scars that only the unflinching patience of true love would get past them.

'Well, I'll say it again—what are you doing here, crying in your bedroom? That's not going to solve anything.' He lifted the magazine out of her hands, stared down at the photograph. 'You might think that I'm some old fool, that I don't understand, but I'm not daft. You won't get far if you don't commit to one another properly. And I don't see much evidence of *that* if you're here and he's there.'

Frankie looked at her father. *Really* looked. When was the last time she had done that? He was of a different generation, but maybe he was no less well meaning or principled than she was. Maybe he did truly want the best for her. There were things that mattered to him that she couldn't understand. But she should respect them. For his sake.

'I love you, Daddy,' she said. 'I won't always agree with you, but this time I do.'

He hugged her gruffly, then pushed her away. No time for that kind of nonsense.

'Well, get on with you, then.' He shuffled around, put his hand on the banister and made his way down to the kitchen—to his Sunday lunch and his steady, uneventful life.

'You young people can be awful stupid at times.'

* * *

Rocco turned off the radio. Silenced the preamble to to-day's match. A resounding win predicted for Hermanos Hermida against their old rivals San Como. Dante was captaining for the first time. Rocco was glad. It was time he led the team on his own. He was a much more naturally talented player anyway—always had been. What Dante lacked in bloodthirstiness he made up for in consummate skill. A fearless child, he had excelled in every sport.

Yes, he thoroughly deserved his place—and the win that was predicted to follow.

As for himself…? Rocco wasn't sure when or if he'd play again. He'd wanted to be there today, to lend Dante support. But right now he had come to the end of this particular road.

He sat back, ensconced in the leather bucket seat of his Lotus, tilted his head and closed his eyes.

You'd better get yourself sorted, man. You've just lost the best thing that ever happened to you and you're in danger of losing everything else if you don't dig yourself out of this pit.

Dante's words still rang in his ears.

He'd faced Rocco across the snug—having found him holed up there three days after Frankie had gone—when he'd run out of bags to punch and miles to run. When he'd been left with nothing more than a cluster of bottles to drain as he tried to drink the misery away.

'What do you think she'd say if she could see you now?' He'd looked at the mess on the wall—the vintage red-wine stain now dried and pink. 'Her hero. *Everybody's* hero. God only knows what you did for her to give up on you.'

'What would *you* know?' he'd slurred back at Dante.

'You've never known what it's like to feel misery. Everything lands at your feet. Women, money, success...'

'You think? You think I've never known any pain? That just shows what *you* know. It's always been about you, Rocco. You and your *real* family. Your *real* brother. You never gave a damn about all the times I watched my mother in pain, waiting for news of where you were, never understanding why you'd do anything rather than be with us. And all we did was love you. You threw it back in our faces time and time again.'

He had been angry. Angrier than Rocco had known he could be. He'd sobered up in a heartbeat, watching him.

Dante had gone on, 'And how do you think *I* felt? Did you ever stop to think? Rejected over and over like that? Knowing that I was never going to be good enough for you? That I'd never hold a candle to Lodo's memory? You kicked me in the stomach more times than you'll ever know.'

'I...I'm sorry. Dante—I'm so... I'm just a mess. Not worth your love...'

At that Dante had reared up, his face a furious mask.

'Just *shut up*! Stop your self-pity. You're worth every bit of my love *and* our parents' love. And *her* love—Frankie's. You're just too damn stubborn and blind to see it.'

They'd ended up standing, facing each other like cage fighters. He'd so badly wanted to swing at him. So badly wanted to hurt him. Because he knew he was right. He'd acted terribly. Selfishly.

In the end Dante had walked away, shaking his head. And in that moment Rocco had made his mind up. His life as he knew it was over. He didn't want to be a playboy polo player anymore. He didn't even want to be a horse breeder. He didn't care about any of that. None of it mattered while he was hurting the people he loved. And he loved Frankie so much—so much it killed him to think what he'd done to her.

From the moment he'd seen her he'd loved her. He'd fought against it all these years, but he had. She sparkled, she shone, and she was as pure as a brilliant-cut diamond. She'd brought energy and passion and love to his life. She'd lit up the dark, solemn corners of his heart. She'd set fire to him that night in her bed—a fire that he'd never been able to put out. All the women he'd bedded since had been just an effort to smother that flame. But none of it had worked.

Seeing her at the Campo had just lent oxygen to the embers that had always been there. And he'd known then he'd had a second chance. He'd pursued her relentlessly, not taking no for an answer. She was *his*. He wanted her and he would have her. But only on his terms.

Who the hell did he think he was?

Standing in the wreck of his room, he'd thought about what he'd built up and now cared nothing for—his polo, his ponies, his estancia. She'd come farther than him. She might not have the baubles to show for it, the money, but she was honest. She had strength. Integrity. Compassion. And those were the things he'd suddenly realised he lacked.

He had so much to make up for.

The next day he'd gotten up, cleared up the squalor he'd created and started to sort everything out. He'd called in on Dante. Apologised and shared his plans with him: he was going to bow out of polo, get more serious with life, get more involved in his new businesses. And he was going to meet Chris Martinez. He didn't know how yet—but he was.

And after he'd done all that he was going to get

Frankie. He was going to lay his heart out for her. And if she didn't want him he would understand. He'd understand, but he wouldn't give up. He would prove to her that he was worthy of her. Somehow.

And now things had panned out just as he'd hoped. Even the tracking down of Martinez. The trail had heated up again and he'd stepped forward himself—no proxy. He'd wanted a face-to-face, and he wouldn't be wearing anyone's mask when it happened.

And now he was here. This was it.

To think it was all about to draw to its conclusion after twenty years on a pavement outside a modest villa, sandwiched between two high-rises in Belgrano. With the only criminals in sight the tourist-fleecing café owners.

For two hours he sat there, his fingers making slow drumrolls on the steering wheel. Two hours and then twenty years of hate would be gone. Twenty years of carrying a stone in his heart. Weighted, heavy, dungeon dark. And now, with one simple sighting, he'd stepped up to the light.

One look at the family that exited the dusty sedan and trooped into the house—a fifty-year-old man, his wife, his daughter and an infant that had to be his grandchild—and he knew he was free. Martinez looked aged, haggard. Weary. And suddenly the thrill of the chase was doused. He was finally hauling the past into the sunshine of this moment.

Chris Martinez hadn't caused the economic crash. *He* wasn't responsible for them ending up on the streets, for his father vanishing and his mother's breakdown. Rocco had chosen a path close to the dark side, sleeping on cardboard in doorways with Lodo. Stealing and mixing with criminals had only ever been going to end one way.

The Martinez brothers had been little more than children themselves—young men who'd gone deeper and darker than Rocco. But who knew what would have happened if Lodo hadn't died? If the nuns hadn't taken him in? If Senor and Senora Hermida hadn't shone a light in his life?

Lodo was gone. But there was so much to love and live for—so, so much.

His hand hovered over the car's door handle. It was time. He had to tie up this last knot.

He got out of the car and walked across the street. A tiny fence marked off the front yard from the pavement. He swung open the gate and walked four paces to the door. Gomez, the nameplate said. Knocked.

The young woman opened, the dark-eyed baby on her hip. She recognised him immediately and her mouth and eyes widened.

Behind her loomed her father—Chris Martinez, now Chris Gomez. They stared at one another and Rocco saw acknowledgement, acceptance and fear flit across his haggard face.

'I know who you are,' he said.

Rocco nodded. 'Then, you'll know why I've come.'

Martinez didn't flinch, but he stepped out onto the street, pulled the door closed behind him, shielding his home and his family.

Rocco could smell his fear, could see him digging deep for the strength he'd known he would one day need.

'I've changed.'

He stared at his face—looking for what he'd expected to see. Ugly snarling hate…brutality. But it was just a face.

'So have I.'

'I've watched you for years. I've waited for you to come—I knew you would find me.'

Rocco said nothing. There was nothing to say.

'I never meant for it to happen. I was afraid of them—They gave me a gun...' He dipped his head, shook it. 'I'm sorry,' he said finally, looking up.

Rocco looked into his sunken eyes, at his flabby face, his paunch and, behind the windows, peering out, his family.

'It was for me to forgive you.'

He held that gaze for long, searching seconds. This was the moment he had dreamed of for all these years. And now it was his...just seconds ticking by, two men united by one terrible moment and then separated on their own paths.

'It's done now,' he said, and walked away.

Rocco parked outside the cemetery. The late morning had seeped into noon brightness. The shadows had begun to lengthen. He pulled the tiny battered photograph from its leather frame. Lodo had lived for such a short time. If he'd survived...? Who could say? But he would treasure the moments they'd had together for evermore.

He should mark his time on earth in some way. A charity cup? A sponsorship? A garden? He would work that out. But now it was time to move into the present. He'd done all he could. He had to grasp his future with both hands—and fast.

He looked at his watch, worked out the time in Dublin. He knew she was there. Just as he knew it was only a matter of time now until he followed her.

But there was no way he could have forced himself back into her life until he'd cleared this path.

He could see that now. Finally. After the massive fight he'd had with Dante, which had almost ended in violence for the first time ever—and it was all thanks to Dante that it hadn't. His long-suffering brother had taken the verbal blows, the emotional abuse, and had walked away before he'd had to defend himself against the physical ones, too. A true brother.

He lifted his phone. His trips to Europe would be even more frequent now, so the jet he'd just bought was more a necessity than a luxury. The flight plan was already lodged: he'd be flying to Dublin later that day. But back to La Colorada first, to get everything organised with the horses. Although Dante was captaining HH, he had a ton of stuff of his own going on, too. Not least with this new mystery woman—the duchess he'd been pictured with on a yacht in the Caribbean.

He'd never known Dante so tight-lipped about a woman. And so sensitive. It made a change...

He pulled out into the midday suburban traffic, the urge to plant his foot to the floor immense. Anything to speed up this journey...the sooner to let his eyes light upon her sweet face.

God, he hoped she'd been okay. That last night— staying apart from her—had been one of the hardest things he'd ever had to do. Knowing that they were both in such pain and not being able or equipped to deal with it. She'd refused every offer of help—even a ride to the airport. But he'd insisted on that. As a concession, he hadn't driven the car himself. A concession that he'd rethought so many times. If he'd actually been at the departure gate with her could he really have let her go?

He didn't think so.

He pulled out onto the highway, sped along. Four hours and then he'd be on the jet. The best sixty million dollars he'd ever spent if he could bring her back home with him.

The straight, sandy driveway, its jacarandas weighted

down with purple blooms, the sky a streak of pale turquoise and the droopy green willows all welcomed him home. He spun the Lotus round and parked with a lot less care than usual. He felt teenager happy. Excited. As if he was going on a first date, but with the stakes so much higher. Incredibly high.

In through the doors and instantly he sensed it.

He stopped. Listened.

Nothing.

Only the steady tick-tock of the irritating antique clock that presided over the mantelpiece in the wide wooden vestibule. Underneath, the unlit fire was flanked by two towering palms in glazed urns. Corridors stretched off in two directions, the sheen of the parquet gleaming with hundred-year-old pride.

Silence.

It was lunchtime. He should be hearing the grooms chattering: the European girls, so highly strung, and all the gauchos—the young ones flirting and the older ones solemnly muttering. But there was nothing.

He walked on through the house. He couldn't dare think the thoughts he wanted to think. But the last time the house had been this silent was when he had thrown everyone out while he went on his three-day bender. And the time before that...

It had been when the staff had given him space. Space to share with Frankie.

He reached the snug, listening like a hunter, feeling as if he was following in the wake of something...of someone. But it was empty. He kept on, his footsteps now falling on the silk runners, deadening all sound apart from the thump of his heart in his ears.

His bedroom. He paused. Put his hand on the brass door plate and pushed. Cautiously he let his eyes fall into the space between the wall and the open door. His eyes landed on the rug, on the shaft of sunlight that lit the floor, moved to the wall by the dressing room. And there sat the tiny battered carry-on bag.

He threw open the door.

He checked the room, the dressing room, the bathroom, went out onto the terrace.

There was no mistake—*no mistake*—none. He picked up the bag and scanned every inch of it. It was Frankie's. He'd know it anywhere. And unless someone was playing tricks with his mind, it could only mean one thing.

Like a wild horse he charged back through the house, powering through doors, changing direction. Back to the snug, where the scent of fresh paint cut through the air. Where could she be? Where the *hell* could she be?

The main doorway was still open as he passed the ticking clock and stepped out into the sunshine, stared out all around. In the distance the grass-cutting tractors were trailing like giant beetles around the cultivated lawns surrounding the lakes. To the left horses grazed, staying near the trees for much-needed shelter.

And then his feet knew where to go, even if his mind didn't. In less than two minutes he'd skirted the house, run past the back terrace to the yard and the stables. Straight to the stalls of Roisin and Orla.

Dante might have chosen them for his string for today's match, but if he hadn't…

He stepped inside.

His heart stopped.

There she was.

Roisin's nose nuzzled into her hand as she turned her huge watchful eyes on him.

Frankie looked up, smiled.

'Hello, Rocco.'

He swallowed. 'Frankie.'

'Hope you don't mind me coming out here to see the ponies.' She ran the backs of her fingers down Roisin's white star. 'I never got a proper chance to get to know them last time.'

She turned her attention fully on the horse, smiled again and kissed her bobbing head, clapped her strong silky neck.

He watched her, transfixed. She was exactly as he remembered—but so different. Her sleek bobbed hair dipped over each cheek, almost obscuring her perfect petite nose and huge honest eyes. Her lips were parted as she murmured a reassuring string of soft words to Roisin. Then they tilted into another smile, which she turned to gift to him.

'You were right. I didn't come here for the horses last time. I thought I had. But it turns out there was a bigger attraction.'

His face eased into a smile. 'I knew it.'

She smiled, so softly, nodded in the half light of the stable.

'It's funny how things turn out, isn't it? Who would have thought that my grumpy old goat of a father would be the one to give me the best advice about love?'

'What advice was that, then?'

He moved closer, cutting out the sunlight that bathed her, casting her slightly into shadow. But she didn't need any sunlight. She *was* sunlight.

Even in the gloom he saw her smile deepen and her eyes sparkle with humour. She turned back to the pony, soothing her with slow, soft strokes.

'He said men can be very stupid sometimes. You in particular.'

He kept pacing towards her.

'Is that right?'

The pony whickered, looking for more affection, but she trained her eyes on his and kept them steady.

'Definitely.'

'He said *I'm* stupid? But I'm not the one who's fallen in love with a bad-tempered, jealous *porteño* with more bumps and scars than a beat-up car.'

She made a face, as if perusing him for the first time. Nodded. 'True, true… You could do with a new paint job.'

The heartbeats that passed were the sweetest of his life. He felt his cheeks almost split as a smile burst right across his face. He took another step closer.

'But he's right. I've been *very* stupid—falling in love with the cheekiest, most smart-mouthed little minx who ever climbed into my bed. Naked.'

'I was looking for something…' This time it was her turn to smile from ear to ear.

'Tell me you found it.'

She smiled coyly. 'Oh, yes. I found it, all right.'

'I think that's the first time I've seen you blush, Frankie Ryan.'

That crackle of heat began.

'It's too dark to see in here.'

'Maybe I just need to get a little closer to be sure, then.'

He was right beside the horse's withers.

'You'll have to wait in line. I came to see Roisin.'

He stepped right up, so they were almost toe to toe. He saw her chest rise as she drew in a sharp breath. Her lips parted slightly. His appetite for her roared into life. The hunger that would gnaw at him forever.

'You'll have all the time in the world to get to know her.'

He scooped his hand around her neck, felt the warm,

supple skin and silken hair. Sweet heaven, how had he lived these days without her?

'Oh, really?' she whispered, tilting her head back, her perfect wet lips opening in invitation.

He accepted. With the slowest, softest, sweetest kiss.

'Oh, yes,' he murmured, against her mouth. 'I'm not stupid enough to let you go for a third time.'

Thoughts of everlasting days and nights with his woman, his wife, swirled in his head—made him dizzy with his love for her.

Roisin stamped her foot. He grabbed Frankie by the hand, led her out into the sunlight.

'Come on. We've got two hours until we need to be at Palermo. It's Dante's first match as captain. He can help us celebrate.'

She stopped, narrowed her eyes at him. 'Celebrate? What…?'

He bumped his brow. 'Of course. How stupid of me.'

There in the middle of the yard she planted her feet like a stubborn mule. Folded her arms and scowled a grin at him.

And he did the thing he never dared hope he would do, but in his mind had been practising for twenty years. He dropped to one knee, held her pale skinny fingers in his hand, slipped the Ipanema ring off her right hand and looked up into that darling face. Her eyes, filled with trust and hope, and now glistening with tears, stared down.

'Frankie Ryan. Sexiest, smartest, kindest woman alive. Will you marry me?'

He touched her ring finger and held the tiny silver Ipanema band poised.

She cocked her head to one side. 'Can I think about it?'

'Will you do what you're told for once? *Please?*' he said, staring up into her smiling, crying face.

She pursed her lips, wiped her hand over her soaked cheeks, nodded her head. 'I actually think this once I can.'

Then he stood and swooped her into his arms. He clutched her to his chest and she clambered to straddle him even as he strode back across the yard to the house and the rest of their lives together.

* * * * *

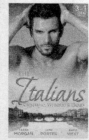

0715_ST16

MILLS & BOON®

MODERN™

POWER, PASSION AND IRRESISTIBLE TEMPTATION

0815/01